Action Hero Fan Girl
Kate Anthony

Action Hero Fan Girl

Kate Anthony

Published by Gryphen Press Publishing, 2019.

This book is a work of fiction. The names, characters, places, and incidents are products of the writer's imagination or have been used fictitiously and are not to be construed as real. Any resemblance to persons, living or dead, actual events, locale or organizations is entirely coincidental.

Copyright © 2015, 2018 Gayle Buck

Pervious title Action Hero Junkie

All rights are reserved. No part of this book may be used or reproduced in any manner whatsoever without written permission, except in the case of brief quotations embodied in critical articles and reviews.

ACTION HERO FAN GIRL

First edition. December 12, 2019.

Copyright © 2019 Kate Anthony.

ISBN: 978-1393605263

Written by Kate Anthony.

Also by Kate Anthony

Action Hero Fan Girl

Chapter One

Mia had always loved action movies. It wasn't for the action, either – though that was good, too. Staring up at the Rock's lovely brown bod, or hearing Arnold snarl, just one more time, "I'll be back!" was nirvana to her. She couldn't help but squirm as Bruce's maniacal laugh pushed past his bloodied lips, or when the Stath's dark menacing glare annihilated his enemies before he kicked their collective ass.

It was all pure, lethal sex appeal.

It was no wonder Mia drooled into her popcorn – big bucket, extra butter, with supersized Coke, in case anyone cared. There was just something about an alpha male. Not that any of them would be comfortable to live with, she reasoned. But for fantasy fare, bring on the testosterone-charged, gun-toting, take-no-prisoners flawed hero with the weird sense of humor.

Mia spent a lot of time at the movies, usually at the late, late shows. She went to work about the time most people were asleep in bed, so that meant her social life was kind of crimped. *Uh, a desert. Like non-existent. Whatever.* This was usually the point in her thoughts that she tried to give herself a good talking-to. *Watch me breezily waving my hand like it doesn't matter.* She snorted to herself. *And if you believe that one, let me tell you about the acre of swampland that'll be perfect for your mom's xerioscape nursery.* She bought a lot of batteries for her personal appliance.

So there she was, minding her own business and chowing down on a bucket of corn, when something really, really weird happened.

The lights went out. Well, theaters were supposed to be dark, but this was way more. THE LIGHTS WENT OUT. No more explosions on screen, no more sound, no nothing.

Just as Mia stood up, about to curse the projectionist, she heard a deep voice yell, "Hit the deck!" Then the splat-splat of bullets and muzzle flares exploded out of the dark, coming from either side of the auditorium.

Mia stood there like a moron, her mouth hanging open and her eyes bugging out.

Something large and hard hit her in the back and down she went, face-first into her smashed bucket of popcorn with extra butter, her front plastered in an icy cold pool of sticky Coke. But Mia didn't mind much the concrete floor. After all, what did it matter when there was a two-ton weight sitting on top of her, squishing the beejezus out of her lungs?

Mia freaked. Mia didn't mind admitting that was what she was doing (knew it but couldn't stop herself). She was wheezing and screaming and wheezing, and the guns were going ack-ack-ack. She'd seen enough action flicks – those were automatic weapons!

Then whoever was sitting on her got off. A big hand grabbed the back of her sweater and hauled her up. "Come on! Come on!" She stumbled to her feet, kind of, because he was yanking her after him. A big, big gun was blasting away from his other hand. Her tongue was frozen to the roof of her mouth.

So the guy threaded them out of the seats, down the stairs in a crouching run, and then out the exit door. It was dark outside, a little chilly, and the cold Coke had stuck her sweater to her front. But Mia was sweating. She wasn't thinking about the weather. Terror did that. Just made the little discomforts sort of go unnoticed.

The guy flung his back against the wall of the building. The gun wasn't barking anymore. The barrel was pointed at the sky. Mia knew this because there was just a little bit of moonlight and it glistened blackly off of the big gun. It was a big, *big* gun.

"We're out!" The guy's voice was really deep. He sounded really focused. He had let go of her; she knew this because both of his hands were on the gun. His body was coiled like a spring, the vague shape of muscles popping out of his arms and large thighs. "They'll follow us! I'll hold them here! You run!"

Mia ran. She didn't stop running. She streaked like a very well-fed deer. Her breasts jiggled and danced. She didn't look back. Her car got larger and larger. Then she got the key out, she was unlocking the door, and diving into the car. Her hand was shaking so bad that it took her two tries to get the key in the ignition. But she did it. Her car was a V8 and it roared when she punched it. Mia was out of that parking lot so fast that she swore she felt Gs.

HE HAD BEEN HIT. THE pain seared his left bicep and he felt the hot splashes of his own blood. It was flowing fast, too fast. He set his weapon down. He had to do what he could to stop the bleeding. He took out his wickedly sharp field knife to slash a piece off the tail of his shirt. Putting away the knife, he labored to wind the scrap of ragged cloth twice around his arm and knot it, pulling the clumsy knot tight with his teeth.

Then he picked up the gun again and waited. He pressed his ear against the surface of the gate and thought he heard sharp voices, but they quickly faded. Stealthily, he laid a hand on the gate to open it, but it didn't budge. He tried again, a little harder, but without result. He cursed under his breath and took a long, slow look around him. He was too exposed where he was. He'd have to go to ground somewhere.

He started out at a fast crouch across the eerie nightscape. Search lights flickered all around but he evaded the cold white beams. The barren field offered little in the way of cover, just a few solitary trees, but he was lucky. He slid down a slick rocky incline, dirt skating from under his boots, and suddenly spotted a darker outline. Cautiously, he moved forward to discover the low overhang of a cave. He crawled inside, pushing his weapon ahead of him. He looked back but could see nothing of the dark sky. That was good. His hiding place wouldn't be readily apparent. He hunkered further back into the black of the narrow cave. Damp, smelly air eddied past his face. He squatted in the mud and rotting debris.

It was cold, but he ignored it. He rested his back against the abrasive rock. His entire left arm was throbbing in pain and it felt weighted down. He closed his eyes, suddenly feeling lightheaded and tired. It had been a near thing, he thought. But at least the woman was safely away. He had watched her run away from him, a flitting, darting graceful figure disappearing into the night. He had been ready to lay down covering fire, but there hadn't been any need. His relief had been overwhelming, especially when he heard the roar of an engine and knew that she had found transportation of some kind.

He recalled the attack, the way the woman had just suddenly appeared in the middle of the exchange of fire, her face terror-stricken, her curvy body frozen in fear. Even in those few scant seconds he had seen how beautiful she was. He had yelled and run at her, tackling her to the mud and covering her body protectively. He hadn't been gentle, not when the bullets were flying so near above their heads. He had hauled her up from the ground, her front plastered with mud and slop, and pulled her after him. She must have been out of her mind with fear, but she had gamely run with him as he wove a way through the dark, dangerous alleys. It had been sheer luck to find that broken gate in the wall. The woman had been able to slip away then.

Unfortunately, that had been the last of his luck. Things had gone to shit. He had lost all communication with his unit. The compromised gate had been discovered and reinforced. He was alone and wounded in enemy territory. The extended blood loss was affecting his mental sharpness. He shivered uncontrollably. *It shouldn't be this cold in this latitude.* Dawn would come all too soon. And with it would come danger

AT HOME, MIA FLIPPED on the TV. She cruised the channels, but there was nothing about a shooting at a local theater. "Shit!" She told herself to stay calm. "Okay, Okay. That makes sense." The police would want to keep a lid on things until they figured out what had happened.

She was still shaking. She decided that a nice hot shower would feel good about then. Besides, she was wearing mashed popcorn and Coke. Not her best look.

By the time Mia got out of the shower, she was feeling a lot calmer. She got dressed for work in her cute adorable greens, except they weren't green, they were pink with yellow flowers on them. As usual, she worked the last RN shift at the hospital. It was a normal night on her floor. No guns blazing, har-har, she thought sardonically.

When Mia let herself in to her apartment again, it was broad daylight and she was bushed. But she hadn't been able to get out of her head what had happened, so she flipped on the TV again. And again, there was nothing! That pissed her off. Here she almost got shot and no one had reported anything about a shoot-'em-up at the theater last night. Mia decided that she was going to go down to the theater and see what she could find out on her own. She grabbed her purse and left, still dressed in her scrubs.

The theater was just opening for the morning premier. There weren't too many people there yet. Mia looked around the lobby and she even went down the hall to the auditorium that she had been in the night before. When she put her hand on the handle, a shiver went down her back. She just couldn't go in there. Other people were, though, and Mia couldn't get over how calm they were. Didn't they know that there were bullet holes in the walls, maybe a yellow police tape to mark a crime scene?

She went to find the manager and started to explain why she was there. "Last night I was watching the flick in #12 and –"

"I apologize, ma'am. We realize there was a problem with the film. Let me give you a complimentary ticket that you can use at any of our features."

Mia ended up clutching a free ticket in her hand and felt totally confused. No one was freaked by what had happened. No one seemed to even know about the shooting. She marched over to #12, pulled open the door, and walked inside. The lights weren't dimmed yet, so she walked up the stairs and stared at every foot of the wall. There weren't any bullet holes. Then she walked over to the opposite side and looked at that wall. *Zero. Nothing. Nada.* Mia started freaking again, but very quietly. If she was going crazy, she decided she didn't want to give it away.

Mia left the theater and walked around the building to the exit door that the guy and she had banged through. A chilly breeze caught her at the corner, lifting her hair and making her shudder, and she hugged her arms around herself. She was just kind of glancing around, not really expecting to find anything anymore. Then she looked down at the pavement. It didn't show up much against the asphalt, just dark spots, but she knew what it was. Dried drops of blood. The hair stood up on her head. She had read that could happen but she had never experienced it before. It was a really weird feeling, all those tiny little hairs coming to shivering attention.

Mia spotted some more drops and she walked over. Then, a little further on, some more blood. Okay, she was weirded out. Her heart was hammering. But she went on following the trail across the parking lot to a big concrete flood culvert. Mia skidded down the cement bank and bent over to look inside. She couldn't make out much, except the barrel of a gun pointed straight at her forehead. Mia made some kind of noise in her throat but nothing intelligible came out. Then she heard something else, a sort of rough, rasping breathing. So that made her look past the gun barrel, and in the deep shadows she could make out a crouching man. There was something familiar about the outline of his head and shoulders. "You didn't kill me last night," she remarked. "So, it will be a real bummer if you off me now."

"You." The man shifted. The gun barrel moved so that it didn't point at her anymore and that made her really happy.

"Uh, you mind telling me what you're doing in there?"

"Waiting for dark."

"Oh." Mia thought about that for a minute. "Are you hurt bad?"

A short laugh. "Bad enough. How did you find me?"

"I followed the dried blood."

He muttered what sounded like a really nasty curse. "I can't stay here, then. I need to move."

"I'll get some help." Mia started to straighten.

"No! I can't be seen. Have you got transportation?"

Mia frowned, staring into the shadows at the man. *Transportation? What kind of a way is that to talk?* "I've got wheels, yeah."

"Good. I'm going to need your help in getting out of this locale."

"You are a freak, you know that? I'll go get my car." Mia straightened up, climbed out of the drainage ditch, and walked away to where she had parked her car. All the time these thoughts were going on in her head. *The guy must be a psycho. Maybe he's an escapee from jail.* Well, she'd listened to the news twice now and there hadn't been anything about an escaped convict or a rampaging psycho. *He's got a gun. A big gun. Well, maybe he has a permit to carry a weapon. Uh huh, right.*

Mia parked as close to the opening of the culvert as she could get. Then she opened the back door and skidded back down the concrete slope. When she crouched down, she could see that damn gun barrel again. "You know, that's getting just plain annoying. Come on." Mia heard a hoarse laugh, and then the man started towards her. He came out slowly, ducking free of the drainage culvert. He squinted his eyes, blinking at the sunlight.

She was startled by her first good look at him. Sure, he had black camo streaked over his face and his dull-colored clothes were dirty. But nothing could disguise those blazing baby blues and that chiseled jaw or those big broad shoulders and nice lean hips. She realized she was salivating. *Oh boy, oh boy.* He did have a big gun, and she wasn't looking at the one he carried. The other one – the bulge in the front of his pants – that was the one she was staring at.

Mia didn't have much time to really check him out. He kind of dove into the back seat of her car and drew up his legs so that she could close the door. He tilted his head just above the window, his eyes peering out, and held his gun at the ready. This time it was the big, black, impressive semi-automatic one that riveted her attention. *Yup, big gun.*

Mia got into the car and started driving. Her mouth engaged, sans brain. "So, where you from? I hope you're not bleeding too bad all over my seat. Blood is a bitch to get out. You got a name? Maybe I should take you to the hospital. Or the police station. It's a really pretty day. Not too warm yet." Just making basic conversation, she told herself, not babbling.

"No hospital, no police. I just need a safe house until dark. Take me to your place."

"Whoa!" Mia's eyes whipped up to the rearview mirror. She was so surprised that she even tapped the brakes. She heard him grunt when he hit the back of her seat. "Sorry about that. No, I don't think that's a good idea. I mean, I think the police can help you better than anyone."

There was that double-damned gun barrel again, pointed right at the back of her head. She drew a breath, while her hands tightened on the steering wheel. "Okay, then. My place."

Luckily, there was no one around when Mia got back to her apartment. Her neighbors all worked during the day while she was sleeping. Mia had never more bitterly regretted her lack of social life. She unlocked her apartment door. The guy muscled her out of the way and went in fast, his gun pointing first one way and then the other. "Okay, you first." Mia sighed and shut the door behind her. "Do you want to check under the bed? Maybe in the closet?"

He just looked at her over his shoulder, his eyes very cold. Then he marched into her bedroom. Mia tagged along behind him. He had a nice butt. He really did check out the closet and under the bed. She wasn't surprised. He also took a quick look in the bathroom and then spun around to pin her with his baby blues.

"We're clear. We'll probably be safe enough for now."

"Yeah, thanks for that." Mia turned around and headed for the kitchen. "I'm hungry. You want something?"

She could hear him following her. Not that he was loud or anything. She could just hear a bare rustle of clothing and his breathing. That short, rasping sound that she'd heard before. Mia stopped dead and turned back around. He almost ran into her. She poked a finger into his broad chest. It felt hard and warm. "You – back to the bathroom. I want to check you out. If you're still bleeding."

"I'll do, ma'am."

"Don't give me that macho crap. Turn your beautiful buns around and march, soldier-boy." Mia scowled up at him just the same as if he was a miffy patient. He gave a ghost of a laugh. He didn't argue but went back to the bathroom. She made him sit on the closed toilet seat. Then she started looking. It wasn't too hard to find where the blood had come from. His upper sleeve was saturated. A strip of ragged cloth was clumsily knotted around his huge bicep. Mia got a mental vision of him pulling the knot tight with his teeth.

Mia got out her emergency kit. It had in it a little more than the usual Bandaids and antibiotic wipes. She took out what she needed.

Mia noticed that he was watching her and that he looked kind of pale. *Must be the lighting.* "Okay, lose the gun. I'm going to cut that rag off. Then you shuck the shirt, so I can see the damage."

He moved kind of slow. He sure didn't want to let go of the gun, but he did. He propped it up against the tub. Mia cut through the ragged bandage with a pair of sharp scissors. It came away stiff in her hand and she dropped it into the trash can. "The shirt."

He pulled the tails out of his pants, unbuttoned the shirt, and shrugged out of it. He had on an A T-shirt underneath. It was sweat-grimed and bloody down one side, but it stretched nicely across that broad chest and molded to a flat stomach. Mia swallowed. She shook her head free of bad, bad thoughts and looked at the wound. It was better than she thought it might be. "The bullet sliced cleanly through the muscle. Looks like it might have nicked the arterial vein. That's why all the blood. You were lucky." Mia cleaned the gaping edges of the torn flesh. Then she threaded a needle. He was looking pale again. "You're not going to faint on me, are you?"

He gritted his teeth. "No! I just don't like needles."

"Rambo would have stitched himself up already."

He lowered his brows and cast a glance of dislike at her. He muttered, "John Rambo is a legend."

"Yeah? Then take a page from the legend's handbook and hold still." Mia began stitching. It took a few minutes. She had to pull together some underlying muscle tissue before she could close the wound and set several neat closing stitches. She tied it off and snipped the thread. Then she covered the wound with a waterproof bandage and taped it. "There you go. A very neat job, even if I do say so myself."

He didn't lift the back of his head from the wall. He just opened his eyes. They glittered at her. Mia didn't think he appreciated her cheerfulness. His mouth was held in a grim, straight line. He looked kind of limp leaning back against the toilet box.

Mia cleaned up everything and put away the emergency kit. She picked up the clean water glass that she always had on the counter, turned on the faucet, and filled it. "Here. You're probably dehydrated. If you feel up to it, get cleaned up in the shower. I can put your clothes in the wash. I'm going to go make something to eat. Come out when you're ready."

Mia left the bathroom, shutting the door behind her.

HE DRANK THE WATER slowly. The cool liquid soothed the tissues of his parched throat, the welcome coolness spreading down inside his body. The nausea receded and his stomach stopped flipping. He set the empty glass down and dropped his skull back against the wall again, breathing heavily. His head was still swimming. *My arm aches like a son-of-gun.*

The last several minutes had taken a lot out of him. The woman had been efficient and quick, but the stabbing of the needle and the dragging together of torn tissue had hurt. It was more than that, though. It was just the *feel* of the thread tugging through his flesh.

He had been lucky. He knew that. Anyone could have found him. The woman had obviously come looking for him in order to help him. It must have taken incredible courage for her to do that, and then to bring him back to her home and care for him. He was grateful and humbled.

She had had the medical supplies and the knowledge to do what she had to do. *She has to be a trained medic.* She had been matter-of-fact and even a little abrasive, with those cracks about Rambo that were obviously meant to stiffen his manly pride. He huffed a grating laugh. It had worked, too. But damn, it had been hard not to squeal and make a few snuffling noises and maybe shed a tear or two!

He worked off his bloodied T-shirt and bent to undo the laces on his dirty combat boots. *Time to get cleaned up.* He'd be glad of a shower after the night he'd had, even if the water turned out to be ice-cold. The water inside the town's environs wasn't always adequate and was often rusty. Shedding his pants and briefs, he stepped naked into the bathtub, glancing down at the drain. No orange discoloration from rust. Either the woman was a maniacal cleaner or she was one of the fortunate ones. He closed the shower curtain and fingered it for a moment, frowning at it. *Pretty pattern, pretty color.*

The building where she lived had looked much better than other places he had seen. It was better kept, not tumbledown or as worn. Apparently, someone who had her skill set was compensated with better living conditions even by the present regime.

He twisted the shower knobs and braced himself for icy spray. A cascade of hot water hit his shoulders and he groaned in sheer pleasure. *Hot damn and hold the sundae!* He had tumbled into heaven.

He found shampoo to wash his hair and then soaped himself down. The water sluicing off of his body was pinkish until the dried blood was washed away. He handled his heavy shaft and balls, cleaning himself briskly, until he suddenly thought of the woman. The incredibly sexy, incredibly brave woman who had saved his life had dangerous curves. His hand slowed and his equipment grew heavier. *She has the most perfect ass.* He envisioned holding that delectable ass in his hands and sliding himself into her heated womb.

He uttered a soft curse. Bracing himself against the tiles with one flattened hand, his shoulders bowed under the splashing water spray, he stroked and jerked himself to completion.

Chapter Two

When Mia got home from working a shift, she usually fixed something for dinner. Then she did some household chores, and maybe read or zoned out in front of the TV or went to the movies, before she got ready for bed. It was kind of a lonely, boring life. *Nothing exciting ever happens to me.* She derisively grimaced to herself. *Poor, poor me. I ought to get a cat.*

Now she had a deranged hunk taking a shower in her bathroom.

Mia calmly put together a one-dish skillet dinner, consisting of hamburger and spicy rice. The aroma of sizzling onions and chili powder and browning hamburger made her mouth water. She opened the fridge and got out a couple of beers. On second thought, she got out another bottle. She'd need two for herself.

He came out wrapped in a blue and orange and pink beach towel. Mia guessed one of her fluffy terry bath towels wouldn't have covered much. Not that she still couldn't tell that he had a nice package. His gold hair was damp. His gorgeous face was clean of camo now, but sported a sexy bad-boy shadow. His manly chest was covered with a dark red-gold mat of hair that narrowed as it descended to his flat belly. And there she was at that package again. Mia grabbed one of the beers and chugged a couple of cold swallows. It didn't seem to do much against the heat in the kitchen.

He was carrying his gun in one hand, his clothes neatly rolled in the other. "I didn't know where to put these."

Mia made a come-hither move with her hand. When she tried to talk, she kind of squeaked and had to clear her throat. "Give them to me." Mia took the dirty clothing. "Uh, there's food and beer. Make yourself at home. I'll be right back." She hurried to the tiny laundry room and quickly shoved the soiled clothing and soap powder into the wash. She whirled the dial. The washer started its chuck-a-chuck-a-chuck dance. Then she hurried back to the kitchen.

He had found plates and stuff, but he hadn't started eating. Mia frowned at him. "What's the problem? Don't you like what I fixed?"

"I was waiting for you."

She melted. *Ah, that is just so sweet. A deranged hunk, wrapped in a frou-frou beach towel, with manners!* "Okay, let's eat."

While he made appreciative *mm-mm* good noises, he looked around again at her apartment. He nodded approvingly. "You've got the curtains all drawn. That's good thinking."

"I sleep during the day. It keeps the sun out."

He grinned like she had made a really funny joke.

Mia waited as long as she could. She hoped it wasn't true about curiosity and the cat, because she hadn't forgotten about the big gun. After all, there it was, leaning against the table. Mia tried not to look at it. "Look, who are you? What happened last night?"

He narrowed his eyes at her. "I shouldn't say anything, but I owe you. I'm Special Ops. You don't need to know about last night, except that you were a civilian in harm's way and I took measures to keep you alive."

"Okay, then. Thanks for that." *So much for conversation.*

Mia removed the dirty dishes from the table and carried them to the sink. He followed and when she looked up, he smiled down at her. His grin was like a one-two punch. Mia practically swallowed her tongue. "Let me wash up. It's the least I can do."

His deep voice finished her. She melted into a gooey puddle. "Uh, sure."

Mia had heard the banging stop, so she knew the wash was done. She pointed towards the hallway. Like an idiot, she crab-walked. She was still pointing. "Uh – I'll go put your clothes in the dryer."

When Mia came back, the kitchen was clean. *Spotless. Better than I would have done.* She wondered if he would leave the toilet seat down.

Mia turned around. He was sitting on her sofa, facing the coffee table, his muscled legs spread wide. She was disappointed that the big beach towel didn't gape that much. She got just glimpses of knotted hairy calves. They were very nice calves. He had taken part of the newspaper and spread it out on the coffee table and his gun was broken down into parts. He was cleaning one of the pieces with a rag and some stuff that Mia guessed had come out of his pack.

"I'm going to go take my shower. I just wanted to let you know."

He glanced up, kind of quick, and his electric blue eyes seemed to flare. But he just nodded, so Mia went away.

Mia didn't take too long in the bathroom. She didn't want to leave her guest by himself. He might feel lonely. She threw on a loose T and some comfortable sweat pants and hurried out to the living room.

The gun was all put back together and was leaning against the sofa. Her hunk was lounging against the corner sofa pillows, one leg straightened out on the cushions, the other leg sprawling over the side of the sofa. He looked gorgeous and tired.

"Why don't you go to bed? You probably need the rest." Mia sat down on the arm of the big stuffed chair that was kind of angled at the side of the sofa. She combed her fingers through her damp, naturally wavy hair.

He shook his head. "Someone has to keep watch."

"I usually stay up for a few hours after I get home. I'll take first watch." *I'll take first watch? How dumb is that?* Mia shook her head at herself. "I'll wake you when I get sleepy."

He got a slow, sexy grin. "Thanks." He sat up and swiveled his body, putting his bare foot down to the floor. The beach towel pulled open and Mia got a real nice glimpse of thick, corded thigh. She was still processing that when he stood up and walked past her. Her eyes widened at sight of the nice flare of flank and butt. "Uh – "

"What?" He stopped and turned. The bulge behind the beach towel was about at her eye level. That close, it looked a little bigger than it had before.

Mia looked up quickly, up the long, long length of his abs and chest and pecs. *God, what shoulders!* When her gaze collided with his electric eyes, she felt a spear of heat sear right down to her toes. "Your gun – " Mia swallowed, tried again. She flapped a hand. "Your gun. You should – should take it with you."

He shook his head. "I must be more tired than I thought. Thanks." He brushed past her again, bent – Mia closed her eyes, then snapped them open again – and straightened with the gun in his hand. He padded past her a second time and her head acted like one of those bobble-head toys. She couldn't tear her eyes away from his hard-as-steel ass. He didn't look back as he walked down the hallway to her bedroom. Mia bent way over the chair arm, craning her neck. *Wait. My bedroom!* Mia snapped upright, nearly giving herself whiplash. Visions of tangled sheets and hot sex careened madly through her head. She snorted at herself. *Like, ri-ight.* "Get a grip!"

Mia didn't remember hitting the TV remote. She didn't really remember what she watched. When she started yawning, she turned off the TV. Then she crept down the hallway to her bedroom.

As she eased the bedroom door open, she wondered what he would do. Actually, she wondered if he would shoot her, but that was really just a tiny thought in the back of her mind. She was too busy hyperventilating, in lust, as she tiptoed over to her bed. "Hey, soldier-boy."

She got no response. She just heard a heavy snore. *Well, damn.* Disappointment didn't begin to cover it. In the dark, she walked to the bathroom and fumbled inside the open door to flip on the overhead. A bar of yellow light fell across the bed. She crossed back across the floor to look down at the man lying under the bedclothes on her bed.

He looked dead to the world. There were dark circles under his closed eyes and now that his face was relaxed, she could see lines of fatigue that she hadn't noticed earlier. All of her lustful inclinations poofed out of existence.

Mia picked up his wrist, her fingers pressed on his pulse. Under her fingertips, she could feel the rapidity of his heartbeat. She frowned down at him. She was a little concerned. He had lost some blood, no doubt about it. His shirt and undershirt had been stiff with it. She laid the back of her hand against his forehead. She could feel the hectic heat of fever. "This is so not good."

She gnawed on her lip, thinking about her options. He hadn't wanted to go to a hospital. There had to be a doozey of a reason for that. Again, the words *psycho* and *escaped convict* sprang to mind. She shook her head, telling herself again to get a grip. She had no reason to think he was either one. Not really, anyway.

Well, I'll watch him. If he gets too bad, I'll call EMS.

If that happened, there would of course be awkward questions that she couldn't answer. But she guessed that would be better than trying to dump a dead body. It wasn't like she could call 1-800-BODY2GO.

Mia checked the bandage on his upper arm, but she didn't see any seepage. *That's a good thing, at least.* She gently laid down his arm and smoothed the bedclothes up over his broad chest. Somehow, touching him that way – to make him more comfortable – made her feel a little tender towards him.

Mia turned off the bathroom light and returned to the living room, leaving the bedroom door open so that she could hear him if he wakened. She'd sleep on the sofa and get up again in an hour or so to check on her crazy-good-looking but nutty patient.

Lying down on the lumpy sofa, she punched one of the cushions into an indented pillow for her head. She pulled a woolly afghan over herself and wriggled around until she was more or less comfortable. She knew she wouldn't get much sleep, so she would be tired when she went back in to work. She told herself it wouldn't bother her too much. She was used to long hours. What she didn't want to think about was what she might have to do if her patient got really, really worse.

He got worse. He was hot and restless.

Mia popped a thermometer into his mouth, one of the instant LED kinds, and read it. His temperature wasn't that bad, but she still didn't like how restless he was. *I can't just go in to work and leave him.*

She decided to call in sick. She was never sick, so she had a lot of sick leave saved up. She pretended that she'd gotten food poisoning. Mia didn't think she was very convincing, but her supervisor bought it.

Her patient slept for a long time. When he woke up, it was like instant on. His eyes just popped open and he was looking up at her. Actually, he was frowning at her. Mia smiled back. It was important to project a positive attitude. "How do you feel?"

He moved around, gingerly flexing his body and stretching his legs back and forth under the covers. Mia watched with interest. His voice sounded gravelly. "I'm okay. What time is it?"

"It's way past second watch. You slept for hours." Mia was feeling really cheerful. He looked a lot better. She offered a glass of water to him and he sat up to drink. The bedclothes fell down to his waist, leaving his naked torso exposed. She looked at his bodacious chest and felt a tingling in parts south. She didn't feel at all platonic towards him like she had a few hours before.

He gave the emptied glass back. Mia set it down on the bedside table. When she looked back at him, she saw that he had narrowed his eyes and he was staring coldly at her. "You should have woken me up." He clenched his jaw like he was biting back some more words, only not the polite kind.

Mia realized he was angry. That surprised her. Then she realized he was still feeling the weakening effects of the wound and resultant illness. For someone like him, an almost perfect human specimen, it must be worrisome that he felt so unlike himself. She spoke soothingly to him, just like any good nurse would. "Look, you lost a lot of blood. You were dehydrated and you probably started suffering from hypothermia after being out like that all night in the cold. You needed the rest."

He looked like he was going to pop off at her, so she popped the thermometer into his mouth. He looked like he might bite it in two, but she shook her head at him. "Be good." Mia took hold of his wrist and they tussled a little bit before he would let her take his pulse. All the while, his electric blue eyes were blazing at her. When she was done with his pulse, she took out the thermometer. His pulse was steady and his temperature was falling back to normal. Mia was pleased and she smiled at him. He narrowed his eyes again.

Her cell phone rang. She plucked it out of her pocket and looked at the caller ID. She flipped open the phone. "Hi, Marti."

"Are you okay?"

Her hunk sat up and reached for the frou-frou beach towel. Mia whipped it away out of his reach. He glared at her. "Oh, sure. Just a touch of food poisoning, I think. Must have been the shellfish."

"Mia, you don't eat shellfish."

He got an evil grin on his face. He reached for the edges of the bedclothes and grasped them, slowly pulling them down past his naval. A narrow, south-heading, line of red-gold hairs was revealed. Mia instantly got that he was threatening to throw off the bedclothes. He was buck naked underneath, of course. It wasn't like she was bashful or anything. In fact, at any other time, she probably wouldn't mind seeing what he had. However, now was so not the time. She didn't want to lose control of her patient.

Mia hurried to end the call. "A bad hamburger. Whatever. Look, I've got to go puke."

"Eeew! Okay – bye!"

Mia snapped the phone shut. Sternly, she leveled her finger at him. "*You're* the one who said no hospital! *You're* the one that got a fever! *You're* the one who couldn't be left by himself, oh no! So *I* had to lie and take off from work. Stop being such a big baby! *Stay in that bed!* Got it?"

"Got it." His intensely blue eyes glittered, like deep lake water struck by bright sunlight. He looked mulish, but he settled against the pillows and pulled the bedclothes back up to his gorgeous chest. Watching that nice flat belly disappear, Mia sighed regretfully. He growled at her. "Who's Marty – Martin?"

"Just my best girlfriend in the whole, whole world! Marti hates her real name – probably because her mom is the only one who calls her Martina." Mia shot a stern look at him as she picked up the water pitcher and poured another glass of water. She palmed a couple of aspirin and offered the glass and the aspirin to him. "I don't like fibbing to Marti or to my boss. You better appreciate it."

He was quiet for a second while taking the aspirin, but he was watching her with eagle eyes. He put the empty glass on the bedside table beside the water pitcher. "You said you had to puke."

"I needed to get off the phone quick." Mia frowned down at him. "You've been trouble from the get-go, do you know that? Men make the very worst patients! Now, get some more rest! You've still got a little fever. I don't want to lie any more than I have to, to cover your pretty ass."

He didn't grin, but she could see the rise of laughter in his eyes. "You're the boss."

"Yeah, hotshot, I am." Mia marched out of the bedroom, mumbling under her breath.

It was a long day. Mia filled in the time by cleaning the apartment and catching up on the laundry and cooking. It was actually kind of fun. It was almost like a mini-vacation because she didn't have to hurry through everything just to get out the door. She sniffed appreciatively.

Her place smelled all lemony fresh, even under the aroma of homemade chicken soup. What was good for the soul was good for the body, too. Especially if it had extra garlic.

Her patient was docile. She only had to scold him once, when he had stumbled into the wall on the way back from the bathroom. She had heard the hard bang and rushed into the bedroom in time to help him safely back into the bed. After she had gotten over her fright and finished giving him a piece of her mind, Mia thought it was a shame that he'd been covered up with the blue and orange and pink beach towel.

ACTUALLY, HE DIDN'T mind staying in the comfortable bed. He felt inordinately tired, so he knew he was still in pretty bad physical shape. He could feel the dying flames of the fever, still licking his bones dry. Yet from time to time, he caught himself shivering with chill under the warm covers.

He had been very, very lucky. He could have bled to death overnight. That shallow cave might have ended up becoming his tomb. Instead, a brave, smart woman had rescued him and patched him up.

Experimentally, he lifted and rotated his wounded arm. He was rewarded with a spasm of fiery pain, so he didn't do it again. Instead, he concentrated on getting better.

He ate when the woman gave him something to eat. He let her take his pulse and his temperature. He made no complaint, even though he had to grit his teeth, when she changed his dressing. Most of the time, he dozed. Other times, he stared at the ceiling, wondering about the woman.

Whenever she came into the bedroom, he felt the way his whole being instantly felt more alive. He tried hard not to show it. He tried even harder to ignore the pleasant sexual tension that she aroused in him, but that was becoming difficult. *I'm a mindless, hopeless, horny idiot.*

MIA THOUGHT HE MUST have hated being regulated to the bed, but he didn't say so. His eyes lit up whenever she came into the bedroom, so she figured he must have been bored out of his mind. He didn't seem to care that she bullied him a little. He just grinned up at her and "yes-ma'amed" her.

Mia could mentally feel herself swooning. *He is just so cute. I'd like to keep him.*

But he was steadily getting better, which meant things were going to change.

When Mia placed his clean, folded uniform and underclothes on top of the dresser in the bedroom, his handsome face was powered up by a big, flashing smile. "I guess this means I can get up soon?"

"Yeah, you're fine. Give it awhile longer and you can dance on out of here." She was caught by surprise by a humongous yawn. "Sorry! I'm going to go get some sleep, okay?" Mia stepped out and closed the bedroom door behind her. As she walked down the short hall, she decided that she couldn't put it off any longer. She had to go back to work. But first, she had to get some sleep. She had been going for almost two days and she couldn't stay up anymore. She collapsed onto the sofa and almost instantly tanked.

When Mia woke up, it was dark. She sat up quickly and looked toward the kitchen. She could see the glow of the digital oven clock and she squinted at it. "Oops!" She scrambled off of the sofa. She hadn't checked on her patient in far too long. *I'm sure he's okay.* Actually, what she was most worried about was that he might already have left. She raced down the hall to the bedroom, pushed open the door, and rushed over to the bed.

Out of the semi-dark, an iron arm swept out and around her, yanking her off her feet. Mia yelped. She landed on the mattress, on her back, the arm still banded around her, and a heavy, heated, very nude male body covered her.

All her inner alarms were going off like crazy. They didn't calm down when warm breath puffed on her face and a deep voice growled, "I've wanted to do this for hours." Then his lips came down hard on hers and her mouth was devoured. Mia managed to pull one arm free and did the only thing a girl could do under those circumstances. She lassoed his brawny neck – and they went at it like French cousins.

A huge hot pike pressed firm against her thigh.

He suddenly heaved up, groaning, and rolled over onto his back. He flung an arm over his face. His chest was heaving a bit. Mia was panting pretty heavily herself. "Sorry! I shouldn't have – "

Her mind was short-circuited, but she still had enough neurons firing to understand he had quit before things were finished. Mia shimmied out of her sweatpants and took hold of the velvety hot joystick. He jerked, his body coming up off the bed, but her bent legs were already grasping his hips. Mia took her seat and let it rip. She had once ridden a mechanical bull. The soldier-boy bucked a whole hell of a lot better. *Yippy-ki-yay!*

It was really, really good. No batteries required.

Mia sank into a deep, contented sleep. But not before she felt his hand smoothing her hair and his weight lifting off of the bed. Her last drifting thought was that she was glad he had second watch.

HE FOUND HIS UNIFORM and underclothes and dressed quickly. He padded barefoot back into the outer room. There were no lights on, but he didn't need any illumination. He had memorized the furniture set up. Without giving it much conscious thought, he moved with easy physical grace through the darkened room.

He approved of the blackout curtains. There would be no one peeping in the windows and no hint of light or movement from inside would leak through. He wondered what kind of life the woman led that required such precautions. He recalled the well-supplied medical kit. Was he just the last in a line of refugees she had helped? She was obviously an American, a civilian. *What is she doing in this backwater country?*

He carefully moved aside a corner of one drape far enough to give a swift glance outside. The sky was edging towards an orange sunset, creating lengthening shadows. He could see the entire sweep of bare ground in front of the building. Not a living thing in sight, just a few parked vehicles. He grunted, pleased, and let the curtain drop. The place was safe enough.

He felt an unexpected peace seeping into him. His body was relaxed but ready for action. The stitched-up wound on his arm barely bothered him. He felt good.

He seated himself in the big stuffed chair and angled his weapon across his knees. It was his turn to stand watch and guard. It was more than a duty. Fierce feelings burned in his chest, protectiveness and frighteningly strong liking. Somehow, the woman curled up asleep in the warm bed in the next room had become more than a hot, convenient hook-up. She was so utterly unlike anyone else he had ever been with. He was beginning to think his life had been turned upside down. *I'd take a bullet for her.*

HER ALARM WENT OFF. Mia put out her hand and groped for the clock, finally slapping the button on the top. She stretched, yawning, feeling all warm and pleasantly relaxed with the aftereffects of her erotic dream.

"You're awake." The deep voice was familiar.

Mia opened one eye to take a peek. *Yep.* There was her erotic dream, leaning against the door frame, dressed in his clean dull-colored uniform. She opened the other eye. He was giving her a slow once-over. Her whole body flash-warmed red. She kind of bunched the sheet in her hand and pulled it up over her bare breasts. *Bare* – She looked down. *Well, I guess I lost my T somehow.*

He was grinning at her, a kind of sexy, knowing grin. His eyes were heated as he stared at her. "You look real pretty, all rumpled and sexy."

Mia swallowed. "Uh, hi." She could have hit herself. Could she have sounded any lamer? She tried again. "I better get up and – and take a shower."

He straightened. His wide hands flexed at his sides. The heat flared hotter in his eyes. For a second, Mia got the impression that he was going to pounce on her. He didn't say anything, but his jaw tightened. He nodded, then spun round on his heel. She heard his rapid tread going down the hallway.

It was obvious that her hunk wasn't at risk anymore. Mia reached for her cell phone on the bedside table. Her supervisor was happy to hear from her. Her regular shift was covered but the emergency room had been slammed and another body was needed, someone who had experience in triage. *That's me.*

It didn't take her long to leap out of the bed and scramble into the bathroom. The toilet seat was down, which made her grin. She showered, shampooed and conditioned, and dried off in twenty minutes. Then she put on her work clothes. Mia stared at herself in the mirror, frowning at her hair while she blow-dried it. She needed a cut, maybe some highlights. She took more time with her make-up than she usually did. *Gorgeous guy in the house – so sue me.* She knew she would have to hustle on the way to work to get there on time.

When she was ready, Mia sucked in a good, deep breath. It didn't help. She was still nervous. Mia went to find the incredible hunk who had given her the most fantastic night of her life.

He had fixed her breakfast. *Okay, cleans up the kitchen.* Check. *Puts toilet seat down.* Check. *Makes breakfast.* Check. *Screws-your-eyeballs blind sex.* Check. Check. He was perfect. Too bad he was crazy.

Mia sat down at the table and looked at the orange juice, scrambled eggs and toast. "This is great!" She picked up her fork and dug in.

He joined her at the table, but he didn't have a plate. Mia looked a silent question, which he actually understood. "I ate earlier." He flicked his fingers in her direction. "You've got scrubs on."

She nodded and swallowed some more puffy-light eggs. The man could cook. "I've got to get to work."

"I don't think you should go out. It could be dangerous."

Mia looked at him over the toast that she had lifted up to her mouth. "It's the last day of my shift. I can't pretend to be sick anymore. Besides, I already called in and I'm really needed. I wouldn't want to, uh, make anyone suspicious by changing my routine." She bit into the toast.

He frowned thoughtfully. "You're probably right."

Mia finished breakfast and carried her glass and plate to the sink. She rinsed the dishes. "You'll be all right here until I get back, right?"

"I don't think anyone will look for me here. I'll be safe enough."

Mia turned away from the sink to look at him. "How are those stitches holding? Do you want me to look at them before I leave?"

His chiseled face softened. "I'm fine. You can take a look and change the bandage when you get back."

She ran to the bathroom to brush her teeth, then into the bedroom to snatch up her purse. She hurried to the front door. "Okay, lock up behind me. I've got a ten-hour shift. I'll see you after."

Before Mia got out the door, he grabbed her close and lifted her high enough that her feet left the floor. His kiss was hard and quick. He set her down, growling in a low voice, "You be safe today."

Her head went up and down, just like a bobble-head toy again. Mia stumbled out of the apartment, shutting the door behind her. She heard the locks slide home. She got into her car and kind of drove off on autopilot.

Mia was almost at work before she realized something really, really important. They didn't know each others' names. "Well, shit." If she ended up dead, done in by a gorgeous Rambo-wannabe, she wouldn't be able to tell anyone who had killed her.

Chapter Three

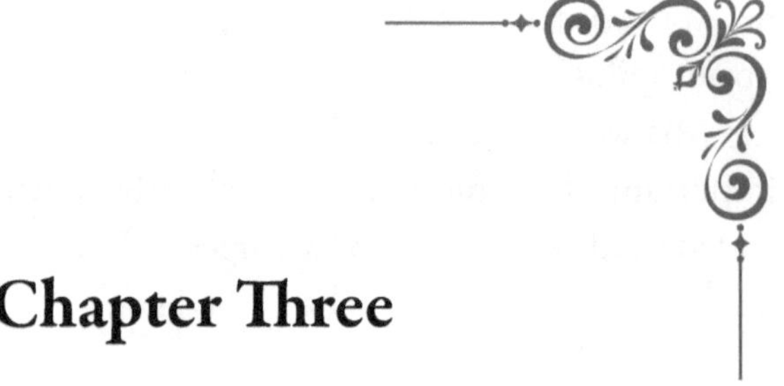

Mia's mind wasn't really on her work. Even when blood spurted from a bleeder and she had to set a clamp, she just got the job done. She didn't let anyone die or anything, but it was just one of those days. Some days, she just didn't want to hear a lot of whining or moaning from sick people. Fortunately, most of them were knocked out with pain medication or sleeping.

She called her best friend, who worked on the same floor she usually did, to let Marti know that she was back but stationed in the ER. Marti came downstairs to sit with her at break and started chattering in her usual cheerful way.

Mia couldn't help it. Her attention wandered. She wondered what her hunk was doing. She knew what she *wanted* him to do – to her. She propped her chin in her hand and drifted into a pleasant, sultry daydream.

Her girlfriend abruptly broke off in mid-sentence. Marti tilted her head, eying her. "What's with you tonight? You act like you're off in your own little fantasy world."

"That's about right," Mia muttered.

When Marti *really* looked at her, Mia could see the wheels spinning. Mia knew that Marti knew that she hadn't really been sick. Marti sometimes could come off as a little flakey. She just had that innocent, naïve, beautiful kind of face. She also had blonde hair. But she was smart.

Marti was scary-smart.

Mia looked at her best girlfriend and debated telling Marti about the weird stuff that had happened to her lately. She kind of edged up to it. "I met this guy at the movies. We had hot monkey sex last night."

Marti's eyes got real round and excited. "*Girl*! You had a one-night *stand*? Meaningless, random *sex* with a *stranger*?" She squealed, hurting Mia's ears.

Well, it was only one night. And he was pretty strange. Mia didn't know anyone else who had gotten shot up in a theater where there hadn't been any bullets flying. "I'm seeing him after shift. I think."

She frowned. *He could leave. He could disappear. I'd never know his name. I'd never walk bow-legged again.*

It was too horrible to think about.

"Details! I want *de-tails*!" Marti's eyes glistened. She didn't get much action, either. Mia thought Marti was a whole lot prettier than her, too. She was normal-curvy. Mia had more bosom – Mia liked thinking of it that way better than saying she had big tits because she thought it was more dignified. Mia also had an apple butt. Only her waist measurement was smaller than her friend's.

"There's not much to tell." But Mia grinned, just to let her girlfriend know she was lying. Marti squealed again and bounced in her chair. So Mia told her about her hot bull ride. Oh, and about a couple of horizontal slow dances, too. When she was done, Marti slumped back in her chair, fanning herself with her hands. "You lucky girl! I am just so *jealous!* A man in uniform, too!"

"Yeah, but Marti – he hasn't said, but I get the feeling he's not going to stick around long."

Marti nodded, looking wise. "Special Ops. You've got to expect that. They can get orders to ship out at any time."

"Yeah." Mia felt herself sink into deep gloom. She stared down at the pitted formica table top and heaved a mournful sigh.

"Ah, Mia. Don't look like that." Marti consolingly patted her arm. "You're off for the next two days, right? So make the most of it."

Break was over and they both hurried back to their stations. Mia usually loved working the ER. It could be such an adrenaline rush, all the blood and broken bones and screaming. This time, she couldn't wait for her shift to be over. She hoped her hunk would be waiting for her.

When Mia finally got home, she inserted her key in the lock. She didn't want to take him by surprise and get shot, so she called out a warning. "Incoming!" She pushed open the door. Someone grabbed her by the arms and her feet left the ground. Mia got a whirling look at her living room. She heard the door slam. Then she was thrown up against it. A hot mouth slammed down, sealing her half-open, astonished mouth. Strong hands flexed on her butt, lifting her up, and lean hips pressed between her thighs. *Whew. Now that's a welcome home, honey.*

He let her slide down. His forehead rested against hers. His hands smoothed circles over her tingling ass. He was breathing hard. Or maybe that was her. Mia couldn't tell. The heat still radiated between them. Her heart was trip-hammering.

He stepped back. The door was Mia's new best friend. It was propping up her melted body. His hot blue eyes glittered at her. "I missed you." There was that growelly deep voice again, the one that sent shivers straight to her toes.

Mia sucked in another breath. *Gotta be strong. Be strong, girl.* She eased away from the door. Her shaking legs held her up. That was good. That gave her confidence. She held out her hand. "Mia Haven."

He looked at her. Then he grinned and stuck out his own hand. Those long, calloused fingers wrapped around hers, very carefully, like he was afraid he might break her hand. "Aiden Smith."

"Well, Aiden Smith." Mia got her hand back. She sort of slid past him, but she didn't take her gaze off of him. "I'm going to take a shower. Just thought I'd let you know." Mia deliberately dropped her purse. She backed up a step. She toed off her sneakers, first one, then the other. She took a step. She pulled her scrub top off over her head, and took another step. Mia dropped her dangling top from her crooked forefinger. Took a couple more steps. With her thumbs, she slid her scrub bottoms down past her navel. Mia stepped back again. She dropped the bottoms and stepped out of the puddle.

All the time, she was walking away from him, sometimes backwards, sometimes looking over her shoulder. Mia watched his electric blue eyes grow hotter and hotter. He brushed a hand across his mouth. Mia slowly traced a fingertip over the edge of lace on her bra. She licked her lips. That was when he rushed her.

He slung her over his shoulder. Mia squealed and bounced against that muscular back. His arm pinned her bare legs against his front. A warm hand was spread wide on her butt. Mia grinned, watching upside down the flex of his magnificent buns. He marched straight into the bathroom.

There wasn't much room. But he lowered her to the floor. Mia felt every inch of his hard body slide over her tingling front before her bare toes touched the cold tile. His thick pike pressed into her soft belly. *It must be awful uncomfortable behind that terrible, confining zipper.* Mia shuddered, deliciously.

"*You drive me mad, Mia!*"

"Yeah, well, you're doing a pretty good job of turning *me* inside out." Mia didn't even know what she was saying. She was too busy pulling his shirt out of his pants. She started undoing buttons and her arms were knocked by his forearms because he was working at his belt and pants.

The rest of their clothes kind of melted away. Then they were standing under the stinging spray doing naughty things to each other. Fingers and tongues and slippery soap and hot body parts. Pretty soon Mia flew apart. *I'm wrung out tighter than the washcloth.*

Aiden carried her to the bed. He laid her down and then lay down beside her. He pulled the covers up over their damp bodies. Mia snuggled up against him, her butt nestling into the warm shallow of his lean hips. She could feel the warm softened bulge pressing against the curve of her rear. His muscular arm came down over her waist, his big calloused hand sliding under and cradling her breast. He didn't say anything about first watch. She was glad.

AIDEN BASKED IN THE warmth of his woman's soft pliant body. Her generous breast nestled in his hand. His hands were big and calloused from handling weaponry. It amazed him that she didn't seem to mind them on her tender flesh. Her womanly scent filled his nostrils like the most seductive perfume. He couldn't remember feeling so content in his life. It felt right, being with Mia Haven. He could let down his guard with her. She made it so easy. She was brave and playful and beautiful. What more could a man like him ask for? If he died tomorrow, he would die happy.

He shifted, spooning her closer, so that he pressed against her from shoulder to thigh. She sighed softly. He adjusted his shoulder and angled his wounded arm more sharply over her supine body. Realization hit him and he lifted his arm into the air, rotating it. He grinned, looking up at the new pinkish scar. *Not a twinge.* He hadn't even felt anything when he had thrown Mia over his shoulder and carried her into the bathroom. Slap on a self-adhesive bandage to protect the still-tender flesh against dirt and he would be good to go. Suddenly, he realized what it meant. His recovery – what it meant to him – to them.

His grin faded. A mingling of desolation and resignation hit him. He was no longer an invalid. His obligation to duty loomed up in the room, like a gray billowing pall of battle smoke. Aiden lowered his arm and folded it back around her, cradling her close. He sighed heavily, regretfully, his breath huffing against her hair. He closed his eyes tightly. For a moment, he pressed his lips against her soft dusky curls. For a moment longer, he pretended. *Damn it. Damn it!*

Reluctantly, he disentangled himself from her body and got up out of the bed. His metal dog tags and the silver medallion he wore on chains around his neck swung forward, then back against his sternum, jangling softly. Mia stirred and rolled over, her eyes blinking drowsily. Under the edges of her lids, her eyes gleamed. He knew she was watching him. For a moment, he stood looking down at her. She lay on her back, one hand curved under her cheek, her curly chestnut hair falling onto the pillow. She was beautiful. He knew he was already memorizing the sight of her, with her lush naked body sated from his lovemaking, because he might never see her again.

He didn't say anything. It hurt too much. He just turned away and went into the bathroom to get his pants on. She didn't say anything or call after him, either. It was like she already knew.

MIA GOT DRESSED IN a T-shirt and jeans and trailed into the kitchen, where the light was on. He had turned around one of the kitchen chairs and was straddling it, his big forearms folded on the top of the back. His chin was cradled on top of his arms. There was a ferocious frown on his face. His dark gold brows were lowered and he held his mouth tight in a grim line. He raised his head and looked up at her with a darkened gaze when she came in. "Mia –"

"Yeah. I know." Mia slowly walked over behind him and pressed herself over his bare back. She put her arms around him, her breasts flattening against his hard muscles. She could feel the heat of his body through her T-shirt. Mia laid her cheek on top of his head. His thick tousled hair tickled her face. "You're leaving."

His fingers closed hard over one of her hands, then he let go. "I've got to."

Mia straightened up. She made herself act all business. "Okay, let me look at the stitches." Aiden dropped his forearms. He got up, turned around, and sat back down. Mia stepped between his spread knees so that she could better see the wound. She peeled back the taped bandage. Her work looked good. It looked more than good, in fact. The stitches had dissolved. The wound was closed and pink and healthy-looking. "You heal quick."

He nodded. His chiseled face tautened and a tic jumped in his jaw. "That's why I can't stay any longer. I'm fit enough to go back into action. I have to leave tonight."

She felt it. She had never before understood that old phrase – 'it feels like a kick in the gut' - but now she did. "This sucks."

He barked a short laugh. "It does." He put his hands on either side of her waist and drew her in closer, wrapping his arms loosely around her, with his large hands pressing warmly across her back. "Ah, Mia."

Aiden buried his face in the turn of her neck and shoulder. Mia felt his firm lips press against her skin. She blinked her eyes rapidly. She sniffed a couple of times.

He lifted his head and his electric blue gaze searched her face. "Mia, sweetheart, don't cry."

Mia brushed her eyes, quick, with the backs of her hands. "I'm not. I won't." *Not until later when I'm alone again.* The forlornness of her thought caught in the back of her throat. She scowled at him and poked her finger in his chest. "You better come back or call me or something!"

"You can count on it." Power backed his firmly spoken promise. His eyes glittered with a savage light. "Even if I have to knock out this whole town to get to you!"

She liked that. It was extravagant and macho and sounded a whole lot better than the evasive I'll-call-you-sometime. She perked up and moved out of encompassing warmth of his embrace. "Good!"

Nothing had changed. He was still leaving. She didn't want to think about that.

Mia glanced around, unsure what to do with herself. So she started bustling around the kitchen, opening the refrigerator, taking stuff out of the pantry. It was good to have an excuse to move around. "I'll make us something nice." She didn't look at him much, but she could feel him watching her. She slapped some pots on top of the stove. "So when are you going?"

"There's time yet. I'll wait until full dark. I'd like to eat first, pull my gear together, spend the time with you." He caught her gaze. "I'm going to need your help again, Mia. I need to get back to where my communications got dropped."

She nodded. She chopped vegetables like a sushi chef. "Okay. I can drive you there."

"I need to get inside. I need to go back in the way I got out. I tried that the other night, after you escaped, but the entrance was barred from the inside."

"Oh. Right! The door can't be opened from the outside." Mia thought it was weird that he didn't want to just buy a ticket, but then maybe he didn't want to be seen at the theater. After all, *someone* shot him. Maybe they were still hanging around. Also, she was pretty sure there were rules about carrying a gun into a theater. Especially a big one. She sure didn't want him to leave the scary thing at her place. So she could definitely see his point about going back in the same way. She set the oven to preheat. "I can probably get the door open from the inside for you."

His eyes narrowed as he considered her offer. "Can you do that? I don't want you to get into any trouble."

"Well, there aren't usually too many people around that late. I don't think anyone will bother me if I open the door, even if they do see me." She shrugged, stirring the bubbling contents of one of the pots she had going. "I don't see what they can say. It's not like I won't have a right to be there. I even have a free pass."

Surprise crossed his face. He laughed, his eyes gleaming at her. "Mia! You're amazing."

"It's no big deal. I'd do it for anyone."

Aiden's smile slowly faded. His electric baby blues seemed to be looking straight into her soul. "I believe you would."

Mia cleared her throat. There was something strange and unreadable in his eyes that made her body feel too warm. She opened the hot oven to slide in the baking dish with the cheese-topped entrée. "There's just one thing, Aiden. You said you dropped your communications. They sweep the place every night."

He frowned, his expression turning thoughtful. "You're right. But I don't have a choice. It's the only way that I can reestablish contact with my team."

She shook her head. She didn't have much hope that a little communication device, or whatever it was he had dropped, would still be in the auditorium. She hadn't even found any bullet holes in the walls. She broke an egg into a bowl, then fished out a bit of shell. She added sugar and milk to the egg. "Well, I can always ask if anything was found the other night."

Aiden's eyes suddenly blazed. The angle of his strong jaw jutted out. "I don't want you involved! I don't want the connection made between you and me. It's too dangerous."

"Relax, soldier-boy! We'll take it as it comes." Mia thought he was making too much out of it, but what did she know. He had saved her life. She *knew* it. Even though there were no bullet holes in the walls. Mia briskly whisked, while she thought about that for a minute. *Yep, I have quietly gone crazy.* Bizarre as it seemed, though, she was really getting a kick out of it. Well, except for the sucky part about him leaving.

AIDEN WATCHED MIA CHARGING around the tiny kitchen, preparing a lavish send-off meal. He counted three pots on the stove and there was something heating in the oven, too. Enticing aromas filled the air, but he didn't feel hungry. His stomach felt a little knotted up like it did before a mission. He'd eat everything just to please her, though. She deserved that much from him.

He swallowed past the unexpected lump in his throat. She was making such an effort! He knew it was all for him. It wasn't just what she was doing with the food, either. It was like she kept reminding herself to smile and so she did. She smiled, but her brown eyes were softened with sadness. Aiden felt his heart constrict. *Ah, damn it, sweetheart.*

He was a member of an elite fighting force, but when it came right down to it, he wasn't as tough as this fabulous woman. She was so awesomely brave, he practically had to wink back tears!

Hiding his own surging emotion, Aiden broke down his weapon and methodically cleaned the already pristine workings. He had the faintest tremor in his hands, which he couldn't control, and for the first time ever he fumbled with putting the well-oiled parts back together. He was glad that his buddies couldn't see his less-than-stellar performance. They'd unmercifully rib him for sure.

THEY DIDN'T TALK MUCH over dinner and cleaning up afterwards. They didn't even say anything when they walked back to the bedroom, undressed, and got back in bed. They made love, slow and sweet, more than once. Then they got cleaned up and dressed again.

Aiden had put on full-uniform. He streaked black camo across his nose, cheeks and chin, until he had turned his face into a startling mask. He carried his pack and his gun out to the living room.

Mia sighed. She blinked back tears. Her heart felt heavy. *He's really leaving.* Slowly, she followed him, dragging her feet. In the living room, she stopped and just looked at him with misery. Muttering a curse, Aiden pulled her to him. Mia whipped her arms around him, pressing herself against his warmth. For a time, they stood there simply clinging to one another. Then he sat on the sofa, gently tugging her down to sit beside him, and put his arm around her. They watched TV. The sitcoms didn't even make them crack a smile. They might as well have been watching Hannibal Lector.

After awhile, Aiden slid his arm out from around her shoulders and got up. Mia mutely watched him. He walked over to the window, lifted a corner of the drape, and peered out. He looked back at her, his black camo-streaked face set in a ferocious scowl. "It's dark."

Mia bit her lip and nodded. It was time for him to go. She passionately wished that she had three wishes.

Mia parked her car pretty close to the side of the theater. Aiden opened the door and slid out, crossing the dark asphalt pavement in a crouched run. He disappeared into the shadows. Mia locked her car and walked around to the front of the theater. She didn't stop at the ticket kiosk but just went on inside. The college-age guy taking tickets was bored. He didn't even look at her. Mia handed over the free pass. He tore it in two and gave her back half. His monotone sounded like crazy Hal in the *Space Odyssey*. "This is good for any feature. Have a good evening."

Mia walked down the hall to auditorium #12. She drew a deep breath and pulled open the heavy swing door. The feature hadn't started yet, but the trailers were running. It was already too dark for Aiden to do any looking around for his 'communication device'. They would have to wait until the feature was over and the lights came up again. Mia glanced up at the rows and rows of empty seats. There were only a couple of kids in the theater, way up at the top. No problem there. She crossed over to the outside exit door and pushed it open. "Aiden?"

He came in quickly, a swift dark shadow. Mia caught a glimpse of the black gun barrel, pointed up. The door closed with a metallic whoosh. His voice growled very low in her ear. *I want you to go now.*

He pushed her towards the outer door. She resisted, digging in her heels. Mia grabbed the rough sleeve of his shirt with both hands. "No way! I'm staying with you as long as I can!"

He snapped a curse. But he didn't argue. He found her hand and clasped it tightly. He held his big gun at the ready in his other hand. "Keep it quiet, then." He was edging them along the auditorium wall when the first exciting scene of the feature, a military helicopter raid on an armed compound in the middle of a sun-drenched town, flashed on the screen. The blinding white light of the first explosion dazzled Mia.

That's when all hell broke loose.

Chapter Four

WHUMP! WHUMP! WHUMP!

The sound was deafening. Wind whipped Mia's hair around her face, the ends lashing her cheeks. Explosions rocked the ground under her feet and she staggered. Aiden steadied her, his hand locking around her upper arm. She could feel the shock impact of his gun conveyed through his body as he fired. "Run!" he bellowed.

Terror stuck her tongue to the roof of her mouth. *This is where I came in the first time!* No time to think. A burst of gunfire rat-a-tat-tatted too freaking close. Mia ducked, her heart trip-hammering, and ran. Aiden pulled her faster. She needed no encouragement. She flew over the ground. *Four minute mile? Ea-asy!* Her laboring lungs felt like they were going to burst.

Blurred blades were suddenly racheting overhead. Aiden gave a massive heave, boosting her upwards. Other hands reached out, snagging her shoulders and arms, hauling her up. Mia felt herself screaming but she couldn't hear herself over the awful noise. She sprawled on a hard metal surface, the impact squashing air out of her lungs. Mia sucked for breath. A metal door slammed shut. *"Clear!"*

Then she was pressed down, on her back the huge hand of gravity. The noise of battle dropped away and there was just the WHUMPWHUMPWHUMP.

Mia was dazed. *I'm on a helicopter. A damn helicopter!* The pieces of her scattered mind started coming back together. *What the freaking hell!*

She felt someone take hold of her, lifting her. She lashed out with her first.

"Mia!"

She stared up wildly. It was Aiden. He was the one holding her. But she didn't want him to. *I want to go back! I want to go home!* She burst into noisy tears.

He pressed her face against his shoulder. His familiar scent – musky sweat and gunpowder – surrounded her. Strangely, she was comforted. He raised his voice, leaning close to her ear, so she could hear him above the noise. "It's okay! It's going to be okay!"

"*Sir? Is the lady hurt?*"

"She's fine. She's just shaken up a bit."

Shaken up? *Shaken up?*

Mia reared straight up, almost clocking Aiden in the chin with the back of her head. He made an *umph* sound, but she didn't pay attention. She was mad, really, really mad. "Shaken up? You nimwit! I've been shot at! Things are blowing up all over! I'm hauled into a helicopter like a sack of potatoes! And I'm just *shaken up a bit*?" Mia slapped the side of his head.

She was glaring but Aiden didn't seem to care. He was grinning at her. Mia heard several weary chuckles. She whipped her head around. That was when she saw there were more men, dressed like Aiden with camouflaged faces, and they were all grinning at her. Even the ones who looked drawn and were sporting bloody bandages.

Mia shut up, but she shot Aiden a really dirty look.

AT MIA'S DAGGER-GLANCE, Aiden grinned. It relieved him that Mia seemed to have recovered somewhat from her fright. *The helicopter came down almost on top of us – like they were looking for us!* He couldn't have planned it better, except for the firestorm that the appearance of the helicopter had generated. That had been a little hairy. He couldn't believe how quickly Mia had reacted. Her instincts had been right on target. She had taken off running straight for the 'copter.

When he had tossed Mia into the helicopter, she had been shaking, practically hysterical. She was obviously terrified at finding herself suddenly in the middle of a running gun battle, and rightly so. Aiden's own heart had been bounding with fear – fear for her. Fear, that she would be hit – he shuddered – or worse.

Those terrible minutes, until they were safe aboard the helicopter, he had cursed himself, up one side and down the other, for getting her into danger. He shouldn't have let her stay with him. He had known how hazardous it could turn out to be. He should have insisted she go home. *But I didn't want her to leave me, selfish bastard that I am!*

Now here she was, wrenched out of her familiar life and thrust into circumstances that had to be frightening to her. Yet she seemed to be handling it all right, now.

Aiden tightened his arm around her. She didn't pull away, but nestled closer against his side. He rested his chin on top of her head. The soft tangled strands of her hair caressed his jaw. He drew in his breath, and he could smell her wonderfully distinctive scent. He smiled to himself and closed his eyes. Almost, he could persuade himself that they were back in her small apartment, shut off from the dangerous world in their own private intimate cocoon.

The familiar clamoring din of the helicopter beat at his ears.

THE HELICOPTER RIDE didn't take long. Everyone got off. Aiden kept Mia close, standing kind of off to the side. He was holding her hand, but he was busy directing things and exchanging laughing quips with the other men. One of the men nodded to her, his dark eyes glinting with amusement. "You've got a handful there, lieutenant."

Mia glowered at him. She wasn't sure, but she suspected he was laughing at her. He walked off, chuckling.

Finally, Aiden was done. He and Mia climbed into a waiting jeep and they were whizzed off towards a silver tootsie-roll shaped building. It looked like she was on a military base somewhere. It looked kind of familiar. Well, a lot familiar. Mia was really puzzled by that. She preferred to think about that smaller weirdness instead of the whole big picture.

Her brain imploded. *Picture? As in – action flick? As in – IN?* The fantastic idea seized hold of her mind. *Oh shit, oh shit.* Mia's heart started thumping like a hormone-mad bunny. *I am officially, certifiably around the bend – lock me up and throw away the key!* She was hyperventilating, gasping for air.

Long warm fingers squeezed her hand.

Mia turned her head. Aiden was looking down at her with his gorgeous electric blue eyes, concern in his expression. He looked so cute when he was worried. She couldn't help but smile. Her racing heartbeat slowed down. She squeezed his hand back, earning herself a blindingly sexy grin. Mia blinked. *Well, maybe crazy isn't so bad.*

The jeep jerked to a stop in front of the building. They got out and went inside the silver tootsie roll. The interior was brightly lit and there were several desks and chairs and tables, all occupied by uniformed personnel, and Mia saw a lot of fascinating electronic equipment. She got the impression of quiet efficiency.

Several people were bustling around, carrying folders marked Top Secret. Aiden snagged one of them and asked a question Mia couldn't hear. The man nodded. "Follow me, lieutenant."

Aiden took her hand again and their guide ushered them to the center of the building, where there was a small area cleared of everything except for a large table covered with some maps. An older man with a stocky build was standing in front of the table, staring down at one of the maps.

Aiden and Mia's guide cleared his throat. "General, sir, Lieutenant Smith is here to report in."

The general abruptly turned around. He had an iron-gray buzz-cut. An unlit cigar was clamped between his big white teeth. His winter gray eyes were cold. "Smith! We thought we had lost you. Good to see you back."

"I'm glad to be back, sir!" Aiden snapped to attention. He had dropped Mia's hand. She stood beside him, feeling kind of awkward.

"At ease, Smith. I'll want a complete debriefing."

"You'll have it, sir."

"Who's this, Smith?" The general barked the question. He was looking straight at Mia and he wasn't smiling. She could feel the coldness of his gaze flicking over her. It was pretty uncomfortable but she tried to look him in the eye.

"She's a civilian medic, sir. She came back for me when I was wounded, got me to a safe house, and stitched me up. She helped me get back to the extraction point."

The general looked at her with approval. The atmosphere turned a degree warmer. Mia cautiously let out the breath that she hadn't known she had been holding. "Good job. Your name, ma'am?"

"Mia Haven." The general nodded and turned his attention back to Aiden. Mia felt like she was no longer on the spot and she relaxed. She looked around curiously. She'd never been in a movie before. She wondered if this was a control center. The general bombarded Aiden with questions, but Mia didn't pay much attention. She looked at the maps. There was one of an island with several flags pinned into it. Half hidden under that map was something that looked like a blueprint. She started to move the map off of the blueprint so she could see it better.

The general slapped his palm down on the map. He stared hard at her, rolling the cigar around between his clenched teeth. Mia got the message. She quickly stepped away from the table, somehow managing to stumble over a big utility cord. Aiden reached out his hand and caught her elbow, steadying her. She gave him a quick, grateful smile. "Thanks."

"You look like you both need some rest. I'll have someone escort Ms. Haven to the VIP quarters. You're dismissed, lieutenant."

Mia edged closer to Aiden and took tight hold of his uniform sleeve. "I'm staying with Aiden." She didn't want to be separated from Aiden. He was the only thing that connected her to home. He was the only thing that connected her with sanity.

The general stared at her. His hard, unblinking eyes regarded her for several seconds. Mia didn't dare speak or move. Finally, his sharp gaze moved beyond her face and his voice was dry. "Fast work, Smith."

Mia quickly glanced up at Aiden. Between the streaks of black camo on his face, she could see the red flush staining his cheekbones. "As you say, sir." He sounded very stiff, maybe even defensive.

The general snorted. "Very well! Lieutenant! Show Ms. Haven to your quarters. She will be your responsibility as long as she is with us."

Aiden saluted smartly. "Yes, sir!"

Shaking his head, the general turned his back on them. Aiden and Mia looked at each other. Aiden grabbed her hand and they hurried to make good their escape.

They left the command center and walked a short distance to a cluster of small buildings that all looked alike. Aiden motioned and Mia turned with him to walk up to the front door of one. Stepping onto the small porch, Aiden opened the door and politely ushered her inside.

Mia stepped past him and he followed her, the wooden door falling shut behind him with a hollow thud. She looked around slowly. The room was divided into living room, by the sofa and matching arm chair and coffee table and TV on one side, and dining room, with the small dining table and four ladderback chairs, on the other. A big circular rug covered the floor. It was a plain, utilitarian place, not a thing out of place, all clean and tidy. She could smell the invigorating aroma of Pine Sol.

Mia turned until she was facing Aiden. They looked at each other, both of them kind of serious, neither of them, obviously, really knowing what to say.

Aiden slowly shook his head. He looked troubled and his wide chest lifted in a long sigh. "I didn't want this, Mia. I wanted you to be safe at home."

"Yeah, well, that makes two of us." Mia lifted her shoulders in a confused shrug. There was a lot going on in her head. She was being tugged in too many ways. She could be safe at home, right now, lying in her own familiar bed. *Alone. All alone, so alone.* But here she was instead, with Aiden, in a scary different world.

Mia wasn't sure what she really wanted, so she just walked forward into his arms. His massively muscular arms closed tight around her. Her cheek pressed against his hard, warm chest, and Mia felt it rise beneath her cheek with his breathing. The sound of his heart thudded solidly in her ear. She felt safe. She felt like she was home.

He eased her back from him and his large hands came up to cup either side of her face. His thumbs brushed her cheeks. She looked up into his eyes. He was looking down at her with the most serious expression. The black camo streaks really added to the seriousness. "You're so very beautiful and brave, Mia. I love you."

The man was delusional. But she didn't try to bring him to his senses. Instead, she gave a breathy-sounding laugh. She didn't know where it had come from. It sounded far too sexy to be hers. "Take me to bed, Aiden."

His electric blue eyes instantly heated. He picked her up in his strong arms, like she weighed nothing – she really loved that part – and carried her through an open door into a small bedroom. He laid her down on a wide bed and then he undressed her and she undressed him. There was lots of murmurings and touchy-feely and then he was hot inside her and Mia was losing her mind.

When Mia floated back into her body, she was tucked against him, wrapped up in his arms with her head pillowed on his lovely hairy chest. His chest was rising and falling rapidly beneath her cheek. He smelled good, all musk and male and expended sex. Her eyes still closed, Mia grinned. She couldn't help it. This was the way coolest thing that had ever happened to her in her life.

"Mia, I don't want us to be apart anymore." His fingers were threading gently through her hair.

It felt very, very nice. She glided her own fingertips over his outstanding pecs and the mat of rough wiry hairs. "I don't want to be apart from you, either."

His fingers went still in her hair. Mia could feel his chest stop moving, before he took a really deep breath. His voice went all deep and rumbly. "Mia! Are you sure? You'll marry me?"

Her eyes snapped open. Mia reared straight up. She stared down at him in shock. "Whoa, soldier boy! Where did that come from?"

Aiden sat up, too. She was momentarily distracted by the flexing of that magnificent manly chest matted with red-gold hairs. "I just asked you to marry me."

Mia shook her head, so hard that she thought her brain rattled. *Wow.* Her brain was still stuttering along on half-batteries and her mouth didn't work much better. "But – but you don't know me! I don't know *you*! We're from two different worlds." *Boy, that was an understatement.*

"I know it's crazy! You're right. I'm Special Ops. My life can be crazy. I never know where I'll be sent." Aiden placed his large warm hands on her bare shoulders. "But, Mia, I'm crazy about *you*! I want you in my life."

"I don't know. I don't know." She shook her head. She was all shaken up. She couldn't think.

His hands tightened on her shoulders. "Mia, are you trying to say that you don't...care about me?"

She looked up quickly at him. His face had gone all stony-looking. His mouth was a tight line. He was looking at her with a fierce light in his eyes. He looked really scary with the black streaks of camo on his face. "Oh God, Aiden! You're the best thing that has ever happened to me!"

He crushed her to him. His lips came down on hers. Mia just kind of melted against him. Then she didn't think anymore while she kissed him back. He had her breathless in seconds.

When he stopped kissing her, he folded her close. One of his hands stroked up and down her bare back. His breath ruffled her hair. "We'll work it out, Mia. I promise you."

She nodded, but she didn't say anything. She couldn't, without sounding crazy to him. *Oh, I'd like to stay with Aiden, all right!* But she was inside of a movie! And she wasn't part of the movie. Wasn't there some sort of cosmic law against that? What happened if she suddenly got zapped home? What if she got zapped home – naked! – and ended up at the hospital or the grocery store? *Okay, okay, let's not fall into a pit.* She should think about the positive. Here she was, in a great movie and a really hot action hero thought he was in love with her and gave her great, hot sex. *Duh!* What was she thinking? *Run the ball, Mia, run the ball!*

Mia raised her head and smiled up at him. She traced Aiden's nicely-shaped jaw with her fingertips. "We'll take it as it comes, soldier boy."

He nodded. He got a goofy, tender expression on his face. "That's why I love you, Mia. You're so damn brave."

Mia felt tears prick her eyes. She swallowed. She tried to be a brave, brave woman and not burst into thankful sobs. How had she gotten so lucky? "You have duties, right? I don't want to just sit around while you're busy doing soldier stuff. What can I do?"

"They're always short-staffed at the field hospital. Would you want to – "

"Perfect. That sounds perfect."

He smiled down at her. "You're amazing. All right, let's get some sleep. We've been up a long time."

Mia moved her hand down into his lap and stroked a certain large, warm part of his anatomy. He sucked in his breath. "I was hoping you'd stay up a little longer."

Aiden chuckled. He rolled her under him. His knees spread her legs open, his lean hips settled over her, and he slid home. Mia gave a huge sigh of contentment. She wrapped her arms and legs around him. She grinned up at him. "Did I ever tell you that I really like rock and roll?"

He laughed again, and then he rocked her world away.

Mia must have fallen asleep afterwards because the next thing she knew, she was being gently shaken. She opened one of her eyes. Aiden was sitting on the bed, smiling down at her. His face was clean and shaven. He was dressed in a fresh uniform. Mia opened both of her eyes. "Oh. You're leaving."

"The general wants to see me. Do you still want to go to the field hospital?"

She sat up. "Yes, will you take me there?"

His gaze slowly dropped to her bare breasts and lifted back to her face. He smiled that slow, sexy smile. "I'd *take* you any where, Mia."

She blushed. Mia couldn't believe it. She never blushed. She grumbled under her breath. He laughed at her. Mia hit him on the shoulder. It was like connecting with granite. "Where's the shower? And my clothes?"

Aiden stood up and offered her a hand. She took it. He lifted her effortlessly from the bed to her feet. *Ooh, I love big muscles!* He pointed. "The bathroom is through that door. I'll get your clothes together and put them on the bed."

"Okay." She walked away from him. She could feel a laser centered on her, like one of those red dots before you get shot. Mia stopped and turned around. She frowned at him. "What?"

"I love looking at your gorgeous ass." His eyes were heated again and his voice was low and rumbly. His hands flexed, like he wanted to grab that part of her.

Mia flushed. "Oh." She stood there for a second, kind of self-conscious. Then she lifted her chin. She pivoted and made like a runway model, swinging her well-rounded hips. She heard a low growl behind her. By the time she shut the bathroom door behind her, Mia was grinning. Her guy was really good for her ego.

She showered and shampooed and shaved. There wasn't any moisturizer or a blow dryer. *Of course not – soldier boy isn't into metro.* She dried off and wrapped herself in the large white towel before she left the bathroom. She might be having great, hot sex but that didn't mean she was going to parade around in her jiggling, bouncing skin. Aiden might not be the only one who lived in this house.

In the bedroom lying on the bed, was a uniform and some underwear and a bra. There were also socks and some nice shiny boots. Everything was smaller than what Aiden would wear. Not that he would wear the bra, of course. "Aiden? Where are my clothes?"

His disembodied voice came from somewhere outside the bedroom. "On the bed. I'm having your own clothes cleaned."

"O-kay." Mia eyed the pants. She knew from experience that pants without elastic waists didn't fit her. If she got them big enough to fit her hips, the waist always gaped open. She always had to have new jeans altered after she bought them. Mia put on the silky bra and underwear. They weren't exactly standard military issue, being Victoria Secret sexy. She shrugged. Maybe they were standard movie issue. Then she dressed in the uniform and the footgear. She looked down at herself. Mia frowned. Everything was a perfect fit. Even the waistband of the pants.

Aiden had obviously found her purse because it was sitting on the bed. Mia snatched up the bag, relieved to have her emergency makeup kit, and returned to the bathroom.

She finished doing her face and fluffed her hair, looking in the mirror.

Mia leaned closer. She couldn't believe what she was seeing. Her make-up was flawless. Her ordinary brown eyes looked smoky and sultry. Her hair, which she believed had been cursed from hell, fell in soft waves without a hint of frizz. It was a fantastic chestnut brown with glinting red highlights. *Boy howdy. I look freaking amazing!* She'd somehow gotten a fairy godmother! If the fairy godmother was small enough, Mia was going to put her in her purse and take her home.

She left the bathroom and went to find Aiden.

Chapter Five

The general had sent a driver and jeep for their use and Aiden and Mia climbed into the military vehicle. The driver hit the accelerator and the jeep took off. Mia was pressed back for an instant in her seat. The warm wind blew back her hair.

Aiden could have walked to headquarters, of course, but instead he chose to ride along to the hospital with her. Mia was glad. It gave her a few more minutes to be with him. She had never experienced separation anxiety before.

Aiden must have picked up on her worry-vibes. "Everything will work out, Mia. I promise." He smiled reassuringly at her, lacing his strong fingers with hers. Mia tried not to worry. There wasn't anything she could do about any of it, anyway.

The driver stopped to drop her off at the field hospital. Mia climbed out of the jeep. Aiden, still seated in the jeep, looked out at her. Concern shadowed his expression. His intense blue gaze searched her face. "You're going to be all right?"

"Of course, I am." Mia managed to bring up an almost normal smile for him. Truthfully, she was terrified of being without him. She didn't know what to expect out of the movie. Maybe it would just blow her right out of the screen into the theater like a giant nougie. *Gross, Mia! You've been around way too many pre-teens!*

"You're not just saying that, right?"

"*Of course, I am.*" She opened her eyes very wide. She broadened her smile, showing all of her teeth in a grinning rictus.

Aiden muttered under his breath, beginning to look wild-eyed. He grasped the side of the jeep and the seat, tensing his whole body, as though he was about to launch himself feet first out of the vehicle. "Wait, Mia!"

Her hunky hero's overreaction pushed her over into laughter. Her nervous qualms disappeared. Mia suddenly felt a whole lot better. She made shooing motions, flapping her wrists and hands. "No, really! I'm going to be fine. Now go to work."

Aiden subsided back onto the seat. He flashed a relieved grin, then motioned to the driver. "Okay, let's go!"

As the jeep roared away, Mia waved goodbye to Aiden. She turned and went inside the base hospital. The smell of antiseptic hit her and she sniffed in appreciation. *Just like home.*

Action movies didn't spend much time showing the inside of hospitals, so she was curious. She stood looking around for a minute. It was a madhouse. Everyone she saw was scurrying around, so she didn't try to stop anyone to ask for directions.

Mia eventually found the duty nurse on her own. "I'm Mia Haven. I'm here to help out."

The duty nurse didn't question her. She just handed Mia a white lab coat and stethoscope. "I'll call for the on-duty physician."

Mia didn't have long to wait. The on-duty physician emerged from one of the brightly-lit corridors like a whirlwind. He was tall, balding, and wore murky green scrubs. He shot a swift, assessing glance over her. Shaking her hand, he almost crushed her fingers. "I'm Dr. Mason. And you are?"

Mia told him her name. "I'm here to help out while I'm on base."

"Good! Come with me. We'll get you started. It's a busy morning." The doctor was walking so fast that his white coat whipped back. Mia had to trot after him to keep up. "So where did you do your residency? Have you been around gunshot wounds?"

Still trotting, Mia corrected him. "I'm a nurse." She told him that she'd trained for two years at a major inner-city hospital, where gunshot wounds and drug deals gone bad victims had been a daily occurrence.

He nodded. "Good. We need experience." A nurse rushed up to him with a chart and a pen. He didn't stop walking. He glanced at the chart, signed it, and gave it back to the nurse. The nurse sped away. "I'll show you the ER."

When they entered the ER, he introduced Mia to the nursing staff. "This is Dr. Haven. She will be working with us temporarily. Show her a good time, folks." He nodded and raced off.

Mia waved her hand in the air. "Uh, I'm a nurse. Not a doctor."

No one paid any attention. It was like they couldn't hear her words.

A nurse beckoned Mia to go with her. They set out at a fast clip. Mia wondered if anyone moved at anything but speed of light. "This way, doctor!"

They entered the emergency room, but Mia hardly noticed. She was too busy sputtering over being called 'doctor' again.

"Oh, this is just great!" Mia knew she was freaking out again. She could tell because her palms were sweating. Dismay made her mind whirl. She'd been promoted. She didn't have the training. She hoped that she didn't kill anyone. *Coming to the field hospital had been a bad idea, a very, very bad idea.*

The nurse nodded at what Mia had said, but she obviously hadn't caught her sarcasm. The nurse glanced around proudly at the shiny, well-lit emergency room. It was bustling with activity. "Yes, we've got a pretty good facility for a field hospital. We can deal with almost anything. But as you can see, we're swamped right now. We've just had a wave of wounded come in."

Mia knew what that meant. "Triage."

Mia guessed that the nurse thought she meant for her to take her there, because the woman nodded. "Yes, doctor." She cut to the right and Mia followed her. Mia didn't bother trying to correct her about the doctor-title. She just hoped that there were real doctors around. Her heart was thudding madly in her chest from dread. *Stress can cause cardiac arrest.*

They entered a chaotic area, full of wounded military personnel. More were being brought in. There was a lot of blood and shouting and rushing around. Mia's nerves settled down. She was in familiar territory. Triage was something she knew and she was good at. You just did what had to be done to stabilize the patient. Then the patients were sent on to emergency for more individual care.

Mia plunged into the work. It was exhilarating. Her brain snapped, crackled and popped. Her hands and her mouth were right in sync. Staff scurried and snapped to with her crisp orders. Mia's heart pounded with the adrenaline rush. It was hours before she looked up. That was when she heard her name. Well, not *her* name, but close enough.

"Dr. Haven! Dr. Haven!"

Mia focused on the nurse's face. The woman was looking at her, wide-eyed. Mia brushed the back of her hand across her perspiring forehead. "What?"

"You're done, ma'am!" There was a peculiar note in the nurse's voice. She sounded awed, but that couldn't be right. Mia was obviously missing something, something important.

Mia looked around the triage area. The flood of wounded was now a trickle. "Oh! All right, then. We've done some good work." She snapped off the latest pair of bloodied latex gloves and dropped them into the trash.

"Yes, doctor. I was asked to tell you that you have a jeep waiting to take you home."

"Thanks. I'll be glad to go get a shower." Mia glanced down at herself. Her once-pristine white coat was covered with blood. Under her clothes, she was sweaty. She probably smelled like a pig. Mia grimaced. She hoped she could get that shower before Aiden saw her. The condition she was in, even her new fairy godmother would have her work cut out for her.

The jeep whisked her back to Aiden's quarters. Mia went in, almost dragging her feet. She wondered tiredly when the nice shiny boots had gotten so heavy. She saw a uniformed man sprawled on the sofa and it wasn't Aiden. He gracefully leaped to his feet. His unreadable dark gaze roved over her. He frowned.

Mia frowned back. He looked familiar. *Oh yeah, the smart-mouth at the helicopter.* "What are *you* doing here?" She was hot and tired and grumpy. She sounded unfriendly and she didn't care.

"You've got blood on your forehead." He pointed at her head.

Mia thought that was really, really rude. He hadn't told her his name. He hadn't said why he was there. He had *frowned* at her.

She scraped with a fingernail at her forehead and felt dried scales flake off. She remembered that she had brushed the sweat off of her forehead before taking off the bloodied glove. "Yeah, well, I just got out of my laboratory. Frankenstein's parts squirted."

He kind of clamped his jaw. He didn't look like he appreciated the joke. *Okay then, no sense of humor.* Mia's temper fled south. He was rude and she was too tired to summon up her company manners. *I sure don't intend to stand here, jawing at him.*

"Look, I don't see Aiden. So you – " She pointed at him, then at the door. "Get out."

He snapped a salute in kind of a snarky way. "Ma'am! I'll just wait outside for the lieutenant."

Mia nodded. "Fine! Do that!" She tromped into the bedroom and slammed the door shut. Her gaze fell on her own clothes, clean and neatly folded on the bed. Somehow, it made her sad. She had been a part of the movie all day. When she took off the dirty military get-up, it would be like it was all over. Tears pricked her eyes. She liked being

Dr. Mia Haven, awesome triage doctor. *I don't want to give up the silky Victoria Secrets lingerie, either.*

Muttering to herself, Mia stripped off the military gear and just dropped everything on top of the discarded boots. Then she went into the bathroom to take a shower. Getting under the steamy spray and washing her hair, her mood perked up. After all, she was still in the movie. She was still with Aiden. So what if she had to put on her familiar, oh-so-not-sexy cotton bra and briefs? As long as he wanted to rip them off, she was good.

Mia stepped out of the humid bathroom, humming. A waft of damp air eddied along behind her. There was no one in the bedroom. Mia dropped the towel she had wrapped herself up in and got dressed in her civilian clothes. She didn't put her sweater back on, though. It was too warm for anything more than her T-shirt, paired with her jeans. She fluffed her damp hair with her fingers.

She heard sounds like someone was moving around in the living room. The bedroom door was shut, but she could hear the rumble of male voices on the other side. Mia recognized Aiden's deep voice when it got a little louder, especially when he said her name.

"I'm not giving up Mia!"

Well, that was enough to snare her attention! Mia tiptoed to the door and laid her ear flat against it.

"Aiden, I know how you feel – "

"No, you don't! I love her. She saved my life. She *is* my life!"

Mia grinned to herself. *Ah, that is just so sweet!* Her smile slowly faded. *But wait just a minute. Give me up? No way, no how.*

Aiden had asked her to marry him. She couldn't do that, of course. But until it was over, no one was going to screw with her fantastic fantasy!

Mia jerked the door open and stomped out of the bedroom. She could practically feel herself breathing out flames. She shot a glance around the living room. Aiden and the other solider stood staring at her, their mouths gaping open like they were in mid-flap.

Mia narrowed her eyes in a lethal stare. *Yup, that snarky, rude, smart-mouth.* The same one she had tossed out on his can. She pointed at the unknown man. "You! I knew you were trouble the first time I saw you!"

She marched over in her bare feet and planted herself in front of him. She had to look way up before her gaze tangled with his hooded brown eyes, but she tilted her head and gave him a glare that should have singed his eyebrows. "Where do you get off telling Aiden to give me up? Huh? Huh?" Mia poked him in the chest several times. It made her finger sore, but she didn't care. "How would you like me to cut you a new one and forget to sew it up?"

"Mia! Hold on." Large, familiar-feeling hands came down on her shoulders and pulled her back. She felt Aiden's hard body standing behind her and she turned into him. His clean, masculine scent filled her nose as she pressed in. His arms closed around her.

Mia's face was practically mashed against him. Her voice came out muffled. "Who is this asshole? Break his arms, Aiden." The warmth of his breath huffed over her hair. Against her cheek, she felt the rumble of laughter in his chest.

"Bloodthirsty little thing, isn't she?" The smart-mouth sounded admiring.

Mia lifted her head and glared over her shoulder at him. "Shut up."

Aiden let her go. He slung one arm over her shoulders. With his other hand, he waved at the other man. "Mia, meet my best friend, Caesar Thomas. He's been watching my back since we were kids."

"Well, Augustus, you can take your advice and slither on back to Rome! Aiden is *my* guy." Mia crossed her arms over her chest. She saw his eyes drop to her breasts, which were pushed up rather nicely under her T-shirt. "Eyes up, soldier-boy!"

He jerked his gaze back to her face. He glowered darkly at her. "My name is Caesar."

"Right. That's what I said. Augustus Caesar." Mia saw that he and Aiden were both looking at her with the same I-don't-get-it expression. She shook her head in disbelief. Military elite and they'd never heard of Augustus Caesar, one of *the* generals of the ages? Even she knew that much! She waved her hands in the air. "You know - crossing the Rubicon? Et tu, Brute? All that Roman stuff?"

Their puzzled expressions didn't change.

Mia gave up. She was getting distracted from the point, anyway. "Never mind! *You!* Tell me why you want Aiden to break up with me. You don't even know me!"

"Yeah, Caesar. Tell her why." Aiden sounded challenging.

Caesar glared at him. "You know it isn't a good idea."

Mia looked at Aiden, but he didn't glance down at her. He held his friend's eyes with a dare-you stare. His chiseled jaw was rock-hard. But he spoke to her. "You're a civilian, Mia, and I'm Special Ops. That's enough reason. Right, Caesar?"

Caesar thrust out his own granite jaw. "You could go off on a mission and never come back. She'd be left alone. You *know* that."

Mia could see the stag horns rattling already. She held up her hands, tapping a football time-out. She glared at Aiden's friend. "Whoa, hold it! I've been alone. I don't like it. Now I have Aiden. Whatever time we have together, I want it. Got it?"

Caesar eyed her for a minute. Then he smiled. "Yes, ma'am. I got it." Mia decided he was actually pretty good-looking when he wasn't scowling. He shifted his eyes away from her and nodded at Aiden. "I'll see you round, Aiden."

"Right."

As soon as Caesar left, Aiden picked her up in his arms. He whirled her around and laughed. Mia was breathless when he set her down. She stared up at his grinning face. "What has gotten into you?"

"I'm so proud of you, Mia! You don't back down for anyone! Caesar likes you, by the way."

She just looked at him. She didn't say so, but she was pretty skeptical. "Yeah? How can you tell?"

"Well, he didn't kill you."

Aiden said it so matter-of-factly. Mia wasn't completely certain he was joking. "Ha-ha. Very funny. What are we going to do for the rest of the day?"

Aiden smiled real slow. His large warm hands slid up her arms, raising shivery goosebumps. "About what you said – "

Mia caught her breath. The heat in his electric blues almost scorched her. "Which was?"

He slid his fingers into the nape of her damp hair and pulled her head back. His eyes glittered down at her. "Let's work on that time together."

"Okay," she whispered, just before his mouth crushed hers.

He picked her up and carried her into the bedroom, kicking the door shut with his boot. Mia's plain white cotton undies didn't bother him. He just tore them off. Then he had his wicked way with her.

It wasn't exactly PG-13.

Chapter Six

It was barely dawn when Aiden wakened her. His arms were still wrapped around her. A warm hand squeezed one of her breasts like it was a ripe melon. The fingers of his other hand played wickedly between her thighs. She was still drowsy, but her body was already stirring to tingly life. Mia said something witty. *"Mmph."*

His thick, hot length slid into her from behind. Mia might have moaned. She wasn't sure. The slow friction was creating good sensations, the kind that made her body hum. He raised her top leg, grasping it behind the knee. He thrust deeper inside her. *"Aiden!"*

He tightened his hold and began to move faster, harder.

Mia's spine arched. *Oh, my stars!*

"God, I love your body," he growled into her ear.

"I kinda got that last night about the third or fourth orgasm," Mia gasped. He was rocking her hard. Her breasts bounced. Flames started licking up quick-time through her body. She was a bonfire about to burn out of control. Aiden was masterfully fanning the conflagration.

"You're going to come again, Mia! And so am I!"

She couldn't argue with a plan like that. She exploded, the tremors of earthquake shaking her. The blaze consumed her. Through the intense rolling heat, Mia felt Aiden coming inside of her.

It was awhile before they managed to roll out of bed and get ready for the day. Mia discovered new, crisp, perfectly fitting military issue clothing in the closet in her size. She was already one contented, sexed out woman. Finding out that she was still in the movie was a bonus.

Her good spirits rose up even another increment when she found the new set of Victoria Secrets matching pink bra and panties. She didn't even have to fight bedhead! Her hair behaved itself, not a frizz in sight. *I love having magical movie-dust sprinkled over me!*

After she gave Aiden a hot, tongue in the throat, bone-crushing goodbye kiss, Mia cheerfully waved him off to do his soldier stuff. He looked like a stunned ox and he was walking kind of funny. She giggled. *Poor guy. Duty called.*

The jeep driver, who had watched with interest the fervent goodbye kiss, grinned at her and winked when she climbed in the jeep. He whisked her off to the field hospital. "Have a good one, ma'am."

"Thanks!" Mia smiled to herself as she strode inside the hospital. She felt happy and confident. She didn't care anymore that she wasn't a real doctor in real life. Here, in action movie land, she seemed to have all of the training and skills she needed. She was looking forward to a good day.

After Mia's shift at the field hospital, she was informed by her jeep driver that the general wanted to see her at headquarters after she'd had a chance to clean up.

When Mia got to headquarters, an aide escorted her to the general's work area. She saw that Aiden was already there. Mia grinned at sight of him, but Aiden didn't smile back. He looked pretty serious. So, Mia rearranged her face to look serious, too. She didn't put her hands on him or kiss him like she wanted to, either. She didn't know what the military protocol was. She might get him into trouble with a public display of affection. *Maybe we'd both get the firing squad, what do I know?*

The aide asked Mia if she wanted a cup of coffee. After working in the field hospital all day, a shot of caffeine sounded good to her. "Okay."

The general greeted Mia with a nod. There was a measure of approval in his expression when he looked at her. "I hear that you did quite a job yesterday, Dr. Haven. I'm grateful."

Mia nodded. All day, she'd had a certain question burning inside of her, so she just blurted it out. "I'm curious, sir. Where did all of those wounded come from? Surely not just from here. It isn't possible."

The general rolled his unlit cigar between his teeth. "You're right, ma'am. Our forces are fighting on more than one front. This base is a catch-all."

Mia thought that made as much sense as anything else. Actually, she reflected, it made a lot of sense, in a weird way. There were a lot of action and military-themed movies. The wounded and dead had to go somewhere off-screen. Mia wondered if she would see any casualties from the thrillers or spy flicks. The Queen's man, 007, always racked up a few. She might even see Bond himself! Mia was majorely juiced. She really, really loved action movies! She grinned, feeling happy with her strange new world. "I feel right at home."

"Much as we need someone like you on a permanent basis, Dr. Haven, you cannot remain here."

Mia snapped back into the moment. She looked at the general. The general stared back, his face expressionless. His cigar didn't even twitch. Suddenly, she was getting a really bad vibe. She shot a look at Aiden. He didn't look very happy and he kind of avoided her eyes. *Uh-oh. Funny, isn't it, how something great can be shit-canned in an instant? And you don't even see it coming.* "What? Why can't I stay?"

The general shook his head. Mia thought she saw a glint of regret flash in his narrow stare, but his jaw was rock-hard. "You worked at the civilian clinic."

"Uh, okay." Mia frowned. *Civilian clinic?* She could only suppose that the general was talking about the hospital. The *real* hospital, in the real world. She was thinking hard, trying to find the logic. She guessed that she had to be explained some way in the movie. It all made a crazy kind of sense, when she thought about it.

The general gestured with his square hand. "You work for that international aid outfit, right?"

Mia lifted the cup of coffee to her mouth. "Mmm." She didn't want to lie. She was a real person stuck in celluloid. She didn't think the general would want to hear that.

The general didn't seem to need her to say anything. "You will be missed. We can't just have you disappear. It would cause all kinds of trouble."

Yuh think? Mia almost rolled her eyes. Yeah, there would be trouble if she didn't show back up in her life. Her apartment manager would miss getting the rent. He always got kind of pissy about little things like that. "I can see how it might, sir."

"I don't want an international incident."

"Of course not, sir." Mia snorted to herself. Like that was going to happen. The movie plot didn't exactly revolve around her, now did it? Aiden wasn't exactly a lead character, while *she* was just a few forgettable minutes on screen. Mia sighed over that unpalatable truth. She took another sip of coffee. It tasted bitter.

"I am glad you are taking this so well, Dr. Haven."

"I think I always knew my time here was limited, general." Mia glanced over at Aiden. He had been silent the whole time. When he saw her looking at him, he gave her a sad half-smile. She felt a twinge somewhere in the vicinity of her heart, but there was a spurt of anger, too. She didn't understand it. She didn't have any reason to be angry at Aiden. *He hasn't said anything! Why doesn't he say something?* She buried the uncomfortable feeling.

The general rolled his unlit cigar some more. He looked at Aiden and he swiveled his boxy head to look at Mia. There was a fierce look in his hard eyes. Then he shook his head. "All right, Smith! Let's get back to work."

The two men turned to bend over the table with the maps. While Mia sipped her coffee, she brooded darkly. It so wasn't fair. She had found this gorgeous, wonderful hunk and she couldn't keep him. *The script sucked.*

After awhile, she started paying attention to what the general and Aiden were talking about. Something about a missing spook. It sounded a whole lot more interesting than her own whiny thoughts. They were debating about some of the details of the layout of the commandant's fortress. Mia put in her two cents. "The barracks faces the west side of the courtyard. The munitions room is directly opposite the barracks."

The general pivoted slowly. He stared at her with his fierce eyes. "You've been inside the compound?"

"Well, no." She didn't think it was a good idea to explain to them that she'd seen parts of the compound on a big movie screen. "But certain things I do know."

Mia stepped up to the blueprint on the table. She looked at it for a minute, getting oriented in her mind. She nodded to herself, satisfied that she had it straight. She pointed. "Yeah, this is the commandant's office. See this window? It overlooks the town. He stands there sometimes. The rest of that wing, the one with the sea view, is the private quarters of the commandant." She made a face. "It's where he takes his women. Sometimes you can hear their screams in the courtyard. And over here –" She ran her fingertip along another side of the blueprint. "There aren't any windows on this side of the building. This must be where prisoners are held."

"You can hear their screams." Aiden repeated her words in a slow, heavy monotone.

Mia looked up quick, to meet Aiden's eyes. He was gazing at her with such a cold, controlled fury that it made shivers run up and down her spine. Mia carefully trimmed the truth. "The soldiers talk in the cantina. Sometimes the women are taken to the clinic – after."

The general and Aiden exchanged an identical grim look. The general's jaw worked and his cigar jiggled wildly. He struck his hand flat against the table. The loud clap made Mia jump. She spilled her coffee, but luckily, it had already cooled. She switched the cup to her other hand and dried her wet fingers on her pants.

"I want this son-of-a-bitch, bad! We'll take the bastard out if the opportunity shows itself. Our number one priority is still to free our man, but our intel is too sketchy. We can't go in on what we've got. We've already sustained too many losses."

Aiden thoughtfully frowned down at the blueprint. "Sir, what we need is someone on the inside, someone who knows the layout of the compound and the routines of the guards."

"Uh, I might be able to help you there." Mia found herself again the target of two pairs of narrowed, sharp eyes. "Do you know of a man called Cadero?"

"Who is he?" The general's voice was rough. He chomped furiously on his unlit cigar.

"He used to be one of the commandant's lieutenants. He hates the commandant's guts."

"How do you know this Cadero can be trusted?"

Mia drew in her breath and gave them the movie back story. She hoped she wasn't messing up the movie by clueing them in. After all, this part was supposed to have taken place a long time before the military action had hit the screen. "Cadero questioned orders. Instead of having him killed, the commandant sent Cadero away for duty somewhere else. When Cadero returned, he found out the commandant had got hold of his sister. She hasn't been seen since – at least, not by anyone I'm aware of – but it's said she doesn't walk now."

The general's face darkened and the lines bracketing his mouth deepened. "What happened then?"

"Cadero went crazy, tried to attack the commandant. He – was beaten up pretty bad, then taken out in a boat and dumped overboard in the harbor. Somehow, he made it back to shore. Some townspeople found him on the beach and hid him."

"So Cadero is in hiding." The general's bushy eyebrows bristled in a ferocious frown. "Do you know where?"

Mia shook her head. "He has friends at the cantina. Not the soldiers, but others, like the bartender."

"He might be the edge we need." The general didn't take long to think about it. He nodded decisively. "Find Cadero for me, Smith."

"There's just one more little thing you might want to know." Mia looked at the general, then at Aiden, then back at the general. "Cadero is really, really mean, and really, really crazy."

"Loose cannon." The general's voice was dispassionate. He shrugged. "We'll have to watch him close, then."

"Sir, I've also got another idea. Mia says the commandant has a habit of standing at the window of his office. What if we put a sniper in the church bell tower?" Aiden took his thumb nail and ran a trajectory line from point to point on the map of the town.

"Just on the chance of getting off a shot? Risky, but I like it." The general gave an approving nod. He smiled, baring his teeth clenched around the cigar. "Good! I'll give the order." The general looked at Mia and she swore that she could see regret in his hard eyes. "You've been a great help in your short stay with us, Dr. Haven. We will miss you. Smith will see that you get back to the clinic tonight."

"*Tonight*?" Mia thought she could feel a part of her drop into her toes that had no business being there. It felt really heavy and she thought it was bleeding.

"I think it will be best. That is all." With a last look at Mia and Aiden, the general turned his back on them. His posture was stiff. Mia knew it would be of no use to argue.

Mia felt numb. Aiden took her arm and urged her to movement. She didn't know what she did with the coffee cup. She might even have dropped it. Without opening her mouth even once, Mia let Aiden guide her out of the headquarters building and into the hot sunlight.

They walked the short distance to Aiden's quarters. Neither one of them said a word. Mia couldn't seem to wrap her mind around it. She had to leave *tonight*. Just before she stepped inside, she looked up at the skies. The sun was already starting to sink, streaking pink and gold across the clouds. They didn't have long. She was shrieking inside. *What happened to my happy-ever-after?*

Mia began to feel frantic. "It isn't supposed to end like this! Not so soon!"

Aiden guided her to the sofa and sat her down. He dropped down beside her. His weight squished the cushion and she fell against him. He took her hand and laced his fingers through hers. He sighed heavily. "Mia, I'm being sent out on a mission. I have to see that you get safely back home before I go."

Mia clutched his hand really hard. "But you proposed to me!" she blurted. "I can't go *yet!*" She had tears in her eyes. She swiped them away with her free hand.

Aiden looked pained. "You've got to know I still want to marry you. That hasn't changed."

"But how? When?" Mia wanted answers, good ones that she could live with. Mia felt like her insides were cracking open and she was oozing out. It hurt, a lot.

Aiden shook his head, slowly. When he looked at her, his gorgeous electric blues looked bleak. He abruptly muttered a nasty curse under his breath. "This is what Caesar was really trying to warn me about."

Mia leaped up. She was furious. She balled her hands into fists. "Don't give me that civilian versus special ops bull, Aiden! I don't want to hear it! Just say what you really mean! You don't want to be with me!"

"My heart is being ripped out of my chest!"

All of her anger deflated. "Oh!" Hot tears spilled out on her cheeks. Mia dropped to her knees in front of him and tried to hug as much of him as she could get her arms around. He hugged her back, really hard.

Mia suspected he might be crying, too. She couldn't see his face because it was pressed against the top of her head.

Then Aiden eased her away from him, his strong hands gentle on her. "Mia, I want you to have this." He reached up and pulled a silver chain out from under his shirt collar. There was a small medallion hanging on it. "It's St. Christopher, the patron saint of travelers and soldiers. Will you wear it for me, Mia?"

Mia nodded, too choked up to say anything. Aiden undid the clasp and then put the silver chain around her neck. The medallion fell in the hollow between her breasts. Mia reached up. She wrapped her fingers so hard around the silver disk that the little carven image indented her flesh. It was a powerful talisman. She was a traveler from out of her own world and Aiden was a soldier. It meant a lot that Aiden had given her the St. Christopher medallion. "Will I ever see you again?" She sounded so pathetic, and knew it, but she didn't care.

Aiden bent down and lifted her right up into his lap. He didn't strain at all. She gulped. She was so going to miss those muscles! Mia snuggled against his broad shoulder. When he wrapped her up in his big arms, she felt his chest rise in a huge sigh. "I'll try, Mia."

She started to cry again. Aiden raised her face and kissed her. Then he pressed his forehead against hers. "Don't cry, Mia. Please. I can't stand it!"

"I'll c-cry if I want to!"

Aiden gave kind of a choked laugh and kissed her again. Mia grabbed his head and opened her mouth, desperate to taste him. Their tongues tangled together. One thing led to another. She clutched him. He clutched her.

Their clothes flew apart and littered the floor.

Aiden and Mia came together like heat-seeking missiles. They rolled around on the rug, knocking up against the furniture. Mia felt the bruises coming up but she didn't care, as long as he made her part of him. Aiden was hard and hot and frenzied. His mouth, his hands, his sex, all branded her. It was heart-slamming – scorching – *explosive*. It was absolutely the best goodbye sex of Mia's life. She had only one coherent thought left.

Damn it, I don't want to get a nice cuddly cat!

Chapter Seven

The first thing Mia knew about 'the plan' was when she went out the exit door of the theater into the night – and Aiden and Caesar followed her. She was startled and suspicious. "What are you doing?"

She watched Caesar scurry lithely across the theater parking lot, his black shadow moving across the moonlit asphalt. His big gun was in his hands. Mia was distinctly alarmed. She pointed after his retreating form. "What is *he* doing?"

"My assignment is to make sure you get home. Caesar will appropriate a vehicle to follow you and me in your car. When I've made certain of your safety, Caesar will use that transportation to bring us back here, where the rest of our team has secured the gate in anticipation of our return." Aiden's emotionless voice was clipped. He was also watching Caesar's swift progress and he also held a big gun.

"This is crazy, Aiden!" Without answering her, Aiden took her elbow and started to steer her swiftly towards her car. He held his gun ready in his other hand. Mia balked, trying to slow down. She needed time to think. "Wait, Aiden! Just wait!"

Aiden urged her on with his hand. He gestured with his gun towards her car. "Come on, Mia!"

It occurred to her that one of the movie features could let out while Aiden was waving that big gun of his around. All of those people walking out into the lighted parking lot, catching sight of a big man with a big black gun. She could just imagine what would happen then!

Panic...911...SWAT. All with Aiden – and Caesar – right in the middle of it. And this was the real world, where the bullets and the blood were real. There wasn't any movie land hospital where dead people were brought in and were miraculously patched up, all ready to fight another day.

She shivered, knowing it was in fear. But she preferred to blame it on the night's cool temperature.

She didn't want to think about what might happen if they stuck around in the parking lot.

Mia picked up her pace. She was dressed in her own clothes, of course, and she decided she was glad for her sweater. She had forgotten she had left the chill of fall behind her. It now seemed a lifetime ago since Aiden had thrown her up into that roaring helicopter.

They reached her car. Aiden let go of her elbow and Mia just stood there, biting her lip in indecision. Aiden went around to the passenger side and waited. Looking at her over the top of the car, he silently nodded down at the vehicle.

Mia tried again to be the voice of reason. "What if the owner of the vehicle comes looking for it? What then?"

"We'll be back in under an hour. It's a calculated risk. Now unlock your vehicle, Mia."

Mia blindly fished for her keys and dug them out of her purse. She felt all huffy. "Oh, great! *Appropriate a vehicle* – you mean steal! He'll be stopped for grand theft auto and it's not like I could post bail, not after everyone sees that big gun of his. The FBI and the CIA and Homeland Security will all be called in! He'll be detained as a psycho or a terrorist or a psychotic terrorist or– "

Mia heard the powerful rev of an engine and looked over the roof of her car. She stared in horror. "He goes to appropriate a vehicle and he brings back a *Mustang?*"

Aiden grinned at her. No black streaks disguised his face, making him look scary, which suddenly struck Mia as weird. "There's an art to hiding in plain sight."

She really looked at him, then, and saw he was wearing a shirt and soft-faded jeans. He looked like an ordinary, uber-hot guy out with his date. Except for the casually hefted semi-automatic weapon, cocked on his hip and pointed at the night sky.

"I give up!" Mia unlocked her car. She and Aiden got in and pulled the doors shut in echoing slams. Mia secured her seatbelt with a click. She noticed that he was just sitting there. *Oh, right! Let's just red-flag a cop!* She narrowed her eyes and barked at him. "Buckle up, Aiden! I *don't* want to get stopped."

He looked surprised, then nodded and set his gun down butt first between his knees. She watched him as he pulled the strap tight across his broad chest and anchored it. Then he picked up the big gun and rested it across his knees. The barrel was pointed away from her.

Mia started the car and shifted, grinding the gears, which made her mad because she knew better. "Well! This is just like old times. Except you aren't threatening to blow my head off!"

Aiden slanted a pained look at her. "Just drive, Mia."

Mia grinned. Even if she was worried about this stupid stunt of Aiden's, she couldn't help that she was beginning to enjoy herself. It just felt right that she and Aiden were doing something crazy like this together.

She glanced in her rear-view mirror. It reassured her to see the Mustang following at a discreet distance. Then another vehicle turned into the lane directly behind her. Red and blue lights started flashing. "Oh no, oh no! I'm not speeding! Why – oh, my God! *Aiden!* You've got to do something about the gun! If they see it, we'll be arrested!"

MIA WAS FRANTIC. SHE looked like a crazed woman, with her wide staring eyes and opened mouth. Her hair even seemed to be standing on end. Aiden quickly glanced over his shoulder through the back window. He cursed softly under his breath when he saw the flashing lights of the patrol. He understood instantly her concern. He understood, too, that she was more afraid for him than for herself. *Brave, brave Mia! You have my heart.* Swiftly, he broke down his weapon by feel and placed the pieces on the darkened floorboard between his feet. Then he eased out his hand weapon out of its holster and laid it alongside his thigh on the seat.

Aiden realized Mia was falling into a panic. That worried him. He hadn't ever known her to show much fear. But she didn't need to worry about him. He could handle himself. He could keep them both safe. "Pull it together, sweetheart! Breathe!"

She gave a sort of jerky nod and noisily sucked in her breath a couple of times through her pursed mouth. "I'm fine! You're fine! Oh, we're going to die!"

By the time Mia had pulled over and stopped her vehicle, he was sitting with open hands on his knees. He warily watched the patrol soldier approach the vehicle. Aiden took note that the man moved with stolid confidence, not the nervous uncertainty of a novice. The man was a professional. Aiden tensed, poised for trouble.

Mia had rolled down the window. When the soldier bent down to speak to her, the man flashed a small light into her face. She blinked, looking half-blinded. Aiden could see the nervousness in her smile. "Good evening, officer! What seems to be the problem? It's a beautiful night, isn't it? A little cool, though. There's a great action movie showing. Have you seen it?"

Aiden tried to keep his face expressionless, but it was hard. *Action movie? What the hell is she babbling about?* As far as he knew, there wasn't a single theater in business in the entire town. The people's access to entertainment wasn't one of the commandant's priorities. Yet intelligence was admittedly sketchy in many areas.

Under his alert awareness, Aiden's mind moved swiftly. Mia had apparently heard of such entertainments being available to the soldiers, either in locations cut off from public access or inside the compound itself. *Wait a minute! Cadero had been sent off somewhere! Maybe that's important!* Entertainment would be one way to ensure loyalty. It would serve as well to channel the ordinary restlessness that was common amongst soldiers of any stripe.

Aiden speculated about what other forms of entertainment the soldiers might be provided with at unspecified locations – booze, gambling, women. *Maybe even cockfighting.* If they could infiltrate civilian spies – perhaps use the intel to create diversions – create confusion at certain designated targets at certain times! They might be able to eliminate some of the effectiveness of the opposition forces! The possibilities for exploitation began to seem boundless.

Aiden felt that he had stumbled on something important. He'd have to bring the matter to the general's immediate attention. However, there was just the small matter of the patrol that had stopped Mia. It would have to be dealt with first. He had to finish his current assignment, and that meant whatever it took to get Mia safely home. He listened narrowly to their conversation in hopes of discerning that subtle hint – that split second – before all hell broke loose.

"Ma'am, did you know you have a broken taillight?"

"No, I didn't! I'm sorry!"

"I'm going to need to see your license." The soldier flashed the small light across her into Aiden's face.

Aiden smiled and lifted his right hand in a friendly wave. Then he dropped his hand back onto his thigh, nearer the hidden hand weapon. He was confident that if he had to, he could draw the weapon, pin Mia against her seat with his stiffened left arm, and shoot the soldier dead through the open window. Then, of course, there would be the inevitable alarm raised and probably a careening car chase through the dark back streets, with multiple shots fired, ending in a few more dead soldiers.

I wonder if Mia knows how to drive – I mean, really drive.

Of course, the situation probably wouldn't get that far out of control. Aiden saw a Mustang slowly cruise past. He knew that the Mustang would shortly come back by from the opposite direction.

The light retreated, as though the soldier had lost interest in him. Aiden released his breath slowly. *It could just be a clever bluff to throw me off guard.* He felt his fingers twitch and he controlled his instinctive movement towards the hidden hand weapon.

The soldier still stood at the open window, his light trained back on Mia.

Mia had been rummaging in her purse. She pulled out a billfold, opened it, and extracted a small card. She handed it out to the soldier. "You're not going to have to give me a ticket, are you? I'd never live it down with my friends. I work at the hospital."

The soldier was shining his light down on the card. "Mia Haven." He looked at her again, his hard face easing into a thin smile. "Sure, I know who you are! I thought you looked familiar. You took care of my sister-in-law's father when he was sick – Martin Velasquez?"

"Oh, yeah, Mr. Velasquez! I heard he had to have some cardio rehab. How is he?"

Aiden listened to Mia and the soldier chatting away like old friends. He was blown away, especially when the soldier returned Mia's identification to her, gave her a stern warning, and walked back to his vehicle. Aiden twisted his head to watch the man get back into the patrol vehicle. He still couldn't believe it. *He never gave me a second glance!*

Mia started the vehicle and eased it back onto the road. She didn't say a word, which considering how much and how fast she had just been talking was odd.

Aiden looked over at her. He saw that her hands were clenched tight on the steering wheel. "You did real good, sweetheart," he said softly. He secured his hand gun in its holster.

She turned her head slightly in his direction. Her eyes glinted in the green light reflecting from the dashboard. "How did you do that – with your gun, I mean?"

Aiden chuckled quietly. "I've had some training." That training had required him to be able to tear down and put back together a weapon in a matter of seconds, blindfolded. He reached down for the parts of his weapon and expertly put it back together. He laid it across his knees.

"Um, are you sure you didn't miss any pieces? I wouldn't want you to forget something important, like maybe the trigger."

Aiden nearly laughed out loud at her wit. She was always coming up with these quirky quips. Almost from the first time he had seen her, and had pointed a gun at her head, she had disarmed him with her swift, dry humor. With sentimental enjoyment, Aiden let his memory replay it. *"You didn't kill me last night. So, it will be a real bummer if you off me now."*

He kept a suitably grave expression on his face as he made her a solemn promise. "I will check for sure that I've got the trigger when we get to your place."

Mia lifted her chin and sniffed. "Don't be a jerk, Aiden."

Aiden grinned widely. Mia's ability to defuse a situation to comedic opera was priceless.

MIA GLIMPSED AIDEN'S easy grin in the dim light. The adrenaline and headiness from spent fear and relief were slamming through her veins. All of a sudden, she was blazing mad clear through. He seemed completely oblivious to the danger they had been in. Well, of course, danger was his profession, she fumed, but still he could at least have looked a little worried. Anything could have happened! That poor police officer, who was just doing his job – he could have been taken out by a *fictional action-hero*! That would have been one for the books!

It wasn't something that could have been explained away, either, and since the cop had been standing there with her license in his hand, it would have been a good bet that questions would have come knocking on *her* door. Naturally, Aiden wouldn't have taken that into consideration! All he had to do was climb back into the movie, along with Caesar, his trusty sidekick.

Mia was still steamed, but her mad was underpinned with anxiety. Being stopped by the cop had taken time. Aiden had said he and Caesar had just an hour's window to get back to the theater.

She wondered what happened after that magic hour was up – maybe the squad on the other side just melted into cinematic goo! Maybe being stopped by the cop had run them so off schedule that the feature would be over too soon and Aiden and Caesar wouldn't be able to get back.

Then she would have both of them camped out at her place. *Oh, wouldn't that be a swell party! Gun parts scattered all over the place and no privacy with Aiden!*

Above all, Mia just didn't want to go home. She hadn't wanted to come back out of the movie at all. Now that she *was* back to the real world, she didn't want Aiden to rush off. She desperately wanted to make love to him again, but with his fast-approaching deadline there wasn't going to be time. He'd leave her and she would be alone again, just her and … Mia ground her teeth.

"I'M THINKING ABOUT getting a cat!"

"What?" Aiden stared over at Mia. He was confused by the non-sequitur. He shook his head. She had never said anything about getting a pet before and why she chose now of all times to talk about it, he didn't understand.

"Yep – a nice...*cuddly...CAT!*"

Aiden started to ask, but then he changed his mind. The snappish quality in her voice warned him off. He carefully shifted in the seat, trying not to draw her attention. He'd learned to trust his finely-honed instincts. A wise man knew when to cut his losses. He'd just chalk the cat thing up to the mysterious workings of the female mind.

It didn't take many minutes longer before they had reached Mia's apartment building. In front of it there were a scattering of parked vehicles. Here and there, light glimmered from behind curtained windows. Mia parked the car and as they got out of it, Aiden could hear the faint, muffled-sounding heavy beat of music from somewhere. It was all so familiar and almost like he was coming home. Despite the dismal reason for his assignment, Aiden felt something coiled inside of him relax.

Mia unlocked her apartment door. She flicked on the light switch and stepped back, so that he could go in first to do a sweep. "Déjà vu," she said quietly.

Aiden stepped inside. He was aware when Mia followed him in and shut the door. The air had a slightly stale taste, as though the place hadn't been opened up in awhile. That was a good sign. The blackout curtains were still in place. He checked through the front end of the small apartment and moved down the hall. It didn't appear to his experienced eyes that anything had been touched or tampered with. *Good. She probably hasn't been compromised by her association with me, then.*

It was hard to ignore the bittersweet feeling of homecoming. He lingered in the bathroom, running a finger down the pretty shower curtain. He caught the lingering scent of Mia's shampoo. A nostalgic smile touched his face as he remembered that first night. Exhausted, hurting – Mia stitching him up. She hadn't cut him any slack. She had impressed the hell out him.

He stopped again in the bedroom. He couldn't tear his gaze from the neatly-made bed as a kaleidoscope of impressions tumbled through his mind. *Mia's face in the throes of orgasm...her laughter...the knowing feel of her hands on his heated body.*

Aiden bit off a low curse. Shaking free of the erotic images, he abruptly turned on his booted heel and returned to the living room, where Mia had opted to wait for him. She was standing in front of the closed door, her arms crossed, which did nice things for her bosom. He thoroughly approved at how nicely her generous breasts were plumped up. However, the saddened expression in her big brown eyes tugged at his heart, so he didn't dwell too long on her delectable rack. "Mia."

He slung his weapon over his shoulder and reached up a hand to her face. He curved his fingers over her delicate skin. *My sweet, sweet woman.*

She let him caress her soft cheek, before turning her head and pressing her lips into the center of his toughened palm. He felt the firm pillow-warmth, and it affected him clear down to his toes and back again and ended in his groin. His blood rushed through his veins. He felt as though he had been punched lightly in the stomach. He sucked in an unsteady breath.

Her words came to him on a thread of air. "It's time to go, Aiden."

"Yeah." Aiden felt emotion threatening to clog him up. He was keenly aware of his semi-hard. He knew there was no time. Yet as much as he wanted to make love to Mia, there was so much more he wanted – things he wanted to say to her. But it was like the words were tumbling around behind a huge dam, and he wasn't able to break through it. Defeated, he cleared his throat. "You be safe."

"Me? *Me?* You're the crazy one! You and Caesar, the big dumb heroes!"

Mia started poking her finger in his chest, which always amused him. *Feisty little wench. God, I love the way her eyes sparkle!* Even now, when he felt like all kinds of low, she was lifting his spirits. He felt his lips twitch up.

She was scowling at him. She poked him again, harder. "I'm going to be listening to the news! I don't want to hear anything about murder-and-mayhem or armed car chases or anything else, do you hear? And I *do not* want to see your sorry behinds in my hospital!"

"Yes, ma'am!" Aiden felt such a stir of tenderness towards her that he could scarcely bear it. His instinct was screaming at him to grab her into his arms. He was afraid that if he did he wouldn't be able to leave her. So instead, he leaned forward and, without touching her anywhere else, kissed her gently. Their lips clung together for an incredible moment, so packed with passion and sweetness.

Aiden forced himself to step back, trying to catch his breath. His heart was thundering so hard that he swore he could feel it banging against the underside of his ribs. It was like he had been running a five-minute mile with a fully loaded pack over mountainous territory and leaping over ravines. *A feather – that's all it'd take and I'd be on my ass!*

Stunned, he stared down into her beautiful, dear face.

Mia stared back, seemingly just as stricken as he was. Her brightened eyes shone like stars. Her soft pink lips were half-parted, as though waiting for him. Her breasts rose quick and fast under her clothing. She fairly glowed with happiness.

Without even realizing he was doing it, Aiden eased closer. *"Mia."*

She suddenly deflated. Her lovely brown eyes filled and large tears slowly started rolling down her face. Mia squeezed shut her eyes. "Go, Aiden! I'll lock up."

Aiden couldn't speak. He stepped around her, opened the door and slipped out. He waited until he heard the locks engage. Then he turned and walked swiftly away to the waiting vehicle, it's engine running. He opened the door and folded himself inside, instinctively angling his weapon to the best position in the cramped space.

Without a word, his friend shifted gears. The vehicle cruised smoothly away from the apartment building. Neither man said anything for several minutes. They alertly watched the night rushing past their windows. All seemed quiet. There were no new patrols to impede them.

"She was crying?"

"Yeah." Aiden noted there weren't many other civilian vehicles out. It had to be near curfew. The stop by the patrol had inevitably delayed them in their mission. Any later, and he and Caesar might not have been able to use the appropriated vehicle for their return after getting Mia back to her apartment.

"Sorry." There was a short silence. Caesar shot a sideways look at him. "Was it worth it?"

Aiden gritted his teeth until the back ones ached. He already missed her. It was like a part of him had been amputated. His gut was churning with the pain. *Every damn second!*

"Then you were one lucky bastard." Caesar unerringly negotiated the darkened streets. He made a couple of turns. They flashed past the point where Mia had been stopped. Caesar revved the vehicle's engine. In the dashboard's greenish light, his hard face was calm. "I thought I was going to have to take out that patrol."

"So did I. They wanted to see identification papers."

Caesar glanced over at him. "You don't have any papers."

"Mia surrendered hers. She just kept talking. It turned out she had treated one of the man's family members." Aiden didn't bother to explain further. The obvious outcome made it unnecessary.

"She's quite a woman."

Aiden didn't reply to that. He simply grunted.

When they had returned the vehicle to its precise former place, Aiden and Caesar made short work of crossing the open ground towards the shadows that hid the gate in the wall. Their weapons were held steady in their hands. Aiden, then Caesar, pressed up against the cold stone wall. Their breathing was even as they took stock of the night. There was no shout of discovery.

Aiden could sense more than see it when his friend shot a measuring glance at him. Caesar's tone was casual. "You okay?"

"Yeah. Sure." Aiden packed as much confidence as he could into that. Neither man would ever discuss it further. Unless, of course, Aiden opened the topic himself or proved that he had lost his edge – in which case, Caesar would kick his ass back into shape. Aiden felt the warm solid comfort behind that knowledge.

Beside Aiden, the metal gate eased open, flickering light escaping through the crack. A hoarse whisper reached Aiden's ear. "There you are, gentlemen. Right on time!"

Followed by Caesar, Aiden slipped through to the other side.

Chapter Eight

Mia was home, safely back to her safe little life. *Alone. Depressed. Miserable.*

She had no spirit for anything. She just kind of went through whatever things each day held by rote. It was no surprise when Marti noticed and naturally, like the great girlfriend she was, she zeroed in on the problem. Marti asked about her and Aiden.

"He's gone." Mia brushed away a stupid tear. It wasn't like the guy was real, after all. She sighed, knowing what an idiot she was. But she couldn't even make herself get mad about it.

"I'm sorry, girl." Marti shook her head. "I'd never fall for a military man. At least you have your memories, right? Is he gone for good?"

Mia's face felt all twisted. "I think so."

"Well, did you take some pictures of him? You know, so you can scrapbook."

Mia looked at her like she was crazy. "Scrapbook? I don't scrapbook. I don't even know what that is. Are you taking another self-improvement class, Marti?"

She looked embarrassed. "It's artistic expression. Anyway, do you have pictures of Aiden? You never did really tell me what he looks like."

"No, I don't have pictures of him." Mia said it real slow, while she turned an interesting thought over in her mind. She could get the movie when it came out on DVD. Then she could look at Aiden, over and over, using her pause button. She felt her spirits rise. Then she brightened up a little more. Her personal appliance might get a good workout, too. "But there's this action flick we can go to and – "

"Oh, Mia! You know how much I *hate* those!"

"You like all of the Rambos!"

Marti widened her eyes at Mia, like it was a no-brainer. "But that's *different*. John Rambo is just so *sexy*."

Mia struggled with herself. She had to practice deep breathing until she was able to abandon the argument. "*Anyway*, in this action flick is a guy who looks just like my Aiden."

"Really? You're not just saying that because you're pathetic and don't want to be alone?"

Mia sighed. "Tell me again? Why are we friends, Marti?"

She grinned. "Ooh, you're serious! Okay, I'll go to the movie with you tonight!" She clapped her hands. "I can't wait!"

"Yeah, me neither."

Marti ordered a large popcorn, but not with extra butter, and a supersized Coke. Mia didn't buy anything but a box of mints. Marti glanced at her a couple of times, but Mia ignored the questioning looks. Marti munched down a couple of handfuls of corn before she couldn't stand it anymore. "Okay, what happened to your usual?"

"I'm on a diet." It was a lie, but Mia really didn't want to tell her best girlfriend that her appetite had shriveled since she and Aiden had split up. That would open up a discussion she didn't think she could bear up under at the moment.

Marti nodded, satisfied. She noshed another handful of popcorn and sucked on the straw in her Coke. Then she sawed the straw up and down.

Mia scowled at the annoying squeal.

Marti pretended not to notice. "I'm proud of you, Mia. I know what kind of will power it's taking for you not to have the popcorn and soda. But if you change your mind, just let me know. I'll share."

"Thanks, Marti." Mia sighed. She didn't eat popcorn without extra butter, but it was still nice of Marti to offer to share. The music blared loud, racing at a fast, exciting tempo, and Mia's attention was riveted. "Oh, the show is starting!"

Marti leaned towards Mia, but her interested gaze was on the screen. "Tell me when you see the guy. Does he look that much like Aiden?"

"Just like his twin." Mia chewed up a junior mint into itty bitty bits. She wasn't in the mood to suck on it like you're supposed to. She should have gotten the jawbreakers. She felt nervous, wondering if it hadn't been a really stupid idea to come to the movie.

Actually, it turned out to be kind of fun to point out to Marti all of the glimpses of Aiden on the screen. Marti enthused about how good-looking he was and even paid him the ultimate compliment. "You know, he could almost be a blonde Rambo."

When she said that, tears came to Mia's eyes. She sniffed in gratitude. "Thank you, Marti. That's the sweetest thing you could ever say."

Marti squeezed her hand. "What are friends for?"

Mia frowned up at the screen. "I don't remember that cockfight...or this warehouse raid with all of the shooting and ...*Oh, my God! Aiden's wounded!*" She jerked upright in her seat, unable to tear her horrified gaze from the screen.

Marti rolled her eyes and giggled. "Oh, Mia! Silly! It's just a movie!"

"Right! Right, just a movie!" Mia hunkered back down in her seat, her heart still skipping. *He wasn't killed – just wounded a teeny little bit!*

Mia kept her gaze glued to the screen. Except for the colorful crowded cockfight and the blazing warehouse raid, the rest of the action movie was going pretty much as she recalled it. She thought it was kind of weird, though. There were more scenes with Aiden in them than she remembered. It was like he had gone from just a bit part as one of the Special Ops team to a meatier role where he had a name and rank. Mia wasn't complaining, but it just seemed weird. Maybe she was just noticing him more now, since she had met him in person.

The credits started running. The lights hadn't yet come up in the theater, but Marti and Mia got up out of their seats. Marti slipped the long strap of her handbag over her head and adjusted the huge leather bag on one hip. "I can see why you think Aiden is so sexy."

Mia picked up her own purse and followed her friend out of the row of seats onto the carpeted stairs. "I'm going to get the DVD."

"That's a really good idea!"

All of a sudden, black shadows rushed them. Mia saw a brown bag thrown over Marti's head. Then a bag was yanked down over her own head and she couldn't see anymore. The bag stifled her. Her wrists were lashed together with thin plastic ties.

Mia was screaming. She heard Marti screaming. She was thrown into some kind of vehicle. Heavy boots came down on her back and legs and held her down.

Mia heard the loud diesel rumble and felt the acceleration as the vehicle speeded away. Her head bounced on the hard surface of the truck bed. *Oh, so not good! Marti doesn't like action movies!*

THERE WAS A STIR IN the command headquarters, a buzz of muffled exclamations, following in the wake of a uniformed aide hurrying towards the center. Reaching the long table piled haphazardly with maps and reports, the aide skidded to a stop. He came to rigid attention. "Sir!"

The general and Aiden had been discussing the successful warehouse raid, resulting in the destruction of the enemy's ammunition supply, and they broke off to turn around. The worried-looking aide who had interrupted them saluted smartly. The general returned the salute and then clasped his hands behind his back. He fixed his cold stare on the aide. "What is it?"

"Sir! We've received a report that a small squad of the commandant's troops have seized two civilians!" The young aide's eyes flickered in Aiden's direction.

Aiden stiffened. He controlled his expression, but he couldn't stop the sudden clenching in his gut. He had a really, really bad feeling. Something had gone wrong. There had obviously been a setback to their mission. Perhaps it had been some of the sympathizers to the revolution who had been seized, perhaps even some of his newly established contacts.

The aide adjusted his earnest gaze firmly back on the general. Carefully neutral, he finished his report. "Two women, sir. Dr. Haven and another unknown to us."

"What?" Alarm exploded in Aiden's chest. He felt like he had taken a direct hit from a mortar shell. Sheer agony undercut his racing thoughts. *I should never have let her go back! I should have known word would get out of my involvement with her!*

Before he knew he had moved, Aiden grabbed the young aide by his shirtfront. He ignored the twinge in his shoulder where the minor wound was covered by a dressing. He pulled the slighter man up on his toes. Shoving his face into the other man's, he bellowed. "Where did they take her? *Where is she?*"

"Smith!" The general ground out a sharp command. "Release him!"

With difficulty, Aiden reined in his fury. He opened his fist. The unfortunate aide plopped down on his heels and began nervously smoothing down his wrinkled uniform. His expression still showed vestiges of alarm. Aiden ground out an apology. "Sorry, sir."

The general grunted, chomping furiously on his cigar, and returned his attention to the white-faced aide. "Now, what else have you got for us?"

The aide straightened his posture. He warily rolled his eyes in Aiden's direction. "Dr. Haven and the other woman were taken into the compound, sir."

A feral growl erupted from Aiden's throat. All of his muscles bunched, popping out like cords in his shoulders and tensed arms as he flexed his fingers. He had to get his hands on his offense weapon. He'd be locked and loaded in seconds. Then he'd show the bad guys why it was a really, really bad idea to lay hands on his girlfriend!

Aiden started to barrel forward. The young aide leaped to the side and hurriedly backed up out of his way. Aiden barely noticed the kid's gymnastics.

The general stepped into Aiden's path, blocking him. Aiden began to go around his commanding officer. "Excuse me, *sir!*"

"Hold on, Lieutenant!" The general's voice crackled. He didn't move except to widen his stance. He thrust his boxy head forward, glaring fiercely, his cigar jutting from between his bared teeth. "I'm not going to have you go cowboy on me! If I have to, I will lock you in the guardhouse until you get your head clear, understood?"

The general held up his hand and gestured and two guards materialized with weapons, ready for their orders. "Well, Smith? It's your call!"

Aiden stopped. He met full on the general's hard gaze. Aiden gave a short nod. He knew he was a second away from having the MPs called out on him. He tried to still the rapid rise and fall of his chest. He was marginally successful, but there was little he could do about the hard pound of his heart. He bunched his hands into fists. "Understood, sir! However, I must make my position clear. I cannot sit by while – "

"I am as fond of Dr. Haven as you are, Lieutenant, and – "

"Begging the general's pardon, but no, you're not!"

The general looked at him. It was a long, level look that Aiden's own hot gaze never wavered under. The general nodded acknowledgement. He even placed a toughened square hand on Aiden's wounded shoulder and squeezed for a brief moment.

Aiden winced.

"Oh! Sorry, lieutenant!" The general lifted his hand. "You're right, son! I'm not as fond of Dr. Haven as you are. But I promise you that we won't just stand by. We'll blow the place apart if we have to!"

"I'm going to hold you to that, general, sir!"

"Now, if we only knew *why* they were taken." The general chomped furiously on his unlit cigar. He shot a querying glance at the aide who was still attentively hovering, but the aide only shook his head. "Hmph!" The general narrowed his eyes in inner meditation.

Aiden stood by, waiting tensely to hear the more experienced man's thoughts. He could barely restrain his impatience. His first instinct was to run to Mia's rescue, all of his weaponry firing at once, but intellectually he knew that was irrational. It would only serve to get him killed. Mia would still be in the hands of that – that –

Aiden's fear for Mia coalesced into a cold, lethal resolve. *If he touches her, I will rip off his head with my bare hands.*

The general abruptly nodded to himself, redrawing Aiden's attention. He spoke decisively. "Dr. Haven is a well-respected medical professional. The commandant will not risk tipping the balance of international opinion by harming her. She must be needed for her medical expertise, perhaps even for our man. As for the other woman – since she was with Dr. Haven, I must assume she is a professional colleague. So, I believe that both women will be treated with reasonable decency."

"That makes sense, sir." Aiden drew in a long breath, feeling some of his tension leaving him. Still, thinking about sassy, funny Mia in the hands of that monster – Aiden clenched his fists again. *I'm the reason she's in danger!*

"Smith, I expect you to keep a clear head."

Aiden wrestled down the resurgence of murderous rage. *The general is right.* He had to keep a clear head, not go kamikaze-blazing to his death. That wouldn't help Mia or anyone else, and would only jeopardize the overall mission. "I will, sir."

"Good! If we only knew exactly where the women are being held!" The general swiveled to the table and looked down, impatiently tapping a blunt finger against the blueprint of the commandant's compound. "Are they sequestered in the commandant's quarters or somewhere else? Is there an infirmary? If so, where is it?"

The general lifted his block-shaped head. His hard gaze speared Aiden. "We must have Cadero! Now more than ever. Talk to your contacts, Smith! Bribe 'em, shoot 'em – I don't care how you do it! Make them understand the urgency!"

"I'm on it, sir!" Aiden saluted smartly and turned on his heel. He was glad to have something concrete to do. He ignored the high attention he was generating as he strode through the corridor of manned personnel stations. His heavy boots struck a swift, pounding cadence against the cement floor. Everyone stared, but not one person hailed him. Even if someone had, he wouldn't have stopped.

Aiden emerged outside into hot sunlight and turned sharply, making for the transportation center. He wanted a driver, a jeep with a mounted gun, a gunner. He also wanted a crate of tequila. *Bribe 'em or shoot 'em.* He had been given his mission. He would see that it was successfully carried out.

MIA'S BODY WAS ALL bruised up when the vehicle finally braked. She rolled a little, grunting when she connected with a tough boot toe. Mia was hauled to her feet. Then she was pulled down off the vehicle and made to walk, rough hands pushing and pulling at her. She breathed shallowly. The heavy bag smelled of dirt and onions.

There was the grate of a key, the creak of a heavy door. Then Mia was shoved forward. Someone was shoved after her. Then the door slammed, the key grated again, and several boots stomped away. There was silence, except for their shared breathing and the drip-drip-drip of moisture.

Mia pushed up on the bottom of the black bag and wriggled her shoulders and was finally able to shove it off. She could breathe freely again, but it was still pitch black. The air was dank and old and smelled of slime.

"Mia?"

She recognized Marti's voice, except it was all trembly and scared-sounding. "Yeah, I'm here. Did you get the bag off of your head yet?"

"No – I'm too scared." Marti sounded like she was swallowing a sob. "I don't think I want to see whatever this is."

Mia sighed. "My bag smelled like onions."

There was a short silence. Marti spoke up, her tone entirely different. "I think I want this thing off of my head now."

"Follow my voice. I'll help you." Mia talked and walked and she could hear Marti stumbling towards her. Then they fell against each other. Mia helped get the bag off. Marti hunched and held onto her tight. Mia wasn't ashamed to be holding onto her, too. It helped not to be alone in the dark.

"Where are we, Mia?"

"We're not in Kansas anymore, Toto." Mia had a feeling she knew exactly where they were and that scared her spitless. "Uh, Marti? I don't want to scare you or anything, but I think a really bad guy has kidnapped us."

Marti squealed. It hurt her ears and Mia snapped at her. "Stop that! You nearly broke my eardrums."

"I'm sorry." Marti was trembling. "I just don't understand. What does someone want with us? We were just watching a movie!"

There was an edge of hysteria to her voice. Mia grabbed her sleeve and tried to shake her. It didn't work out too well since her wrists were tied together. "Marti, don't go ape on me! We've got to keep our cool. We've got to think!"

"Right, okay, you're right. Think, think, think."

Mia rolled her eyes. "I dropped my purse. Do you still have yours?" She knew Marti's handbag had such a long strap that she had to pull it over her head to the opposite shoulder. "Do you have anything we can use?"

"Oh! Let me think." Marti let go of her. Mia heard her rummaging with her handbag. "I have a lighter!"

Mia was surprised and disgusted. "I thought you quit smoking."

"I have. I am." She sounded defensive. "Look!" The lighter came to life, casting a glow up into her face. That flame was the most beautiful thing Mia had ever seen. It looked like Marti had cupped magic fire in her hands, but it was because her wrists were tied together and she was holding the lighter between her fingers.

"Marti, you rock!"

She giggled. Then she moved the lighter around so that they could see where they were.

Mia's spirits plunged. The accommodations definitely were not the Ritz. There was a cot with a bare, lumpy mattress and a stinking toilet. Mia really did not want to take a closer look at the inside of the toilet. Mold covered some of the rough walls and somewhere water was dripping, but it wasn't from a sink faucet. The faint illumination moved, letting their surroundings fade back into the dark.

Mia didn't care. It was depressing.

"Well, look at that!" Marti's voice was indignant. She had moved the lighter higher. When Mia looked at her, she saw that Marti was looking up. So she looked up, too. There was a bare light bulb hanging from the ceiling. "They could have left the light on!"

Suddenly, Mia heard the echoing scrape and tramp of boots. She waved her bound arms. "Quick! Cut the light! Someone is coming!"

"Oh shit, oh shit, oh shit." Marti flicked off the lighter and Mia could hear her fumbling with her handbag. It had to be tough with her wrists lashed together. But still, Mia thought she could have been a little faster.

The boots sounded really loud and close.

"Can't you be faster?" Mia hissed. Sweat trickled down her spine from under her bra.

"Got it!" Marti's voice was triumphant.

The grate of a key sounded, followed by the squeal of rusty hinges. The light bulb overhead suddenly blazed. Marti and Mia froze, like blinded rabbits facing a snake. Two soldiers came into the cell and grabbed them. A third one waited at the door. They were hustled out and made to walk down a long dreary corridor, guns at their backs, while they followed the third soldier.

Mia noticed other cell doors and because it was something to do besides freaking out, she counted them. It wasn't like counting sheep to get to sleep. It didn't have the same effect. But it did calm her racing heart down a bit, which was a good thing.

They were marched up some stone stairs and out into a courtyard. The sunshine was blinding. Mia's eyes teared up and she blinked and squinted. She stumbled over a rough patch on the ground and got a jab in the back with a gun. "All right, all right. I get the point." *Har, har, I'm a real laugh-track.* She noticed she wasn't the only one *not* laughing.

The two women were marched upstairs to the balcony level of the building. They were pushed through an open door and into an elegant office. Mia had seen it before in the movie, of course, but she thought it was even more impressive in person. There was a beautiful huge wooden desk, all scrolly and touched up with gold paint, lots of bookshelves, a nice carpet, an honest-to-goodness crystal chandelier, and red silk drapes at the window. Actually, the window was one of those double-door arrangements, where you can open them and there's a foot-wide balcony with beautiful black metal railings like in the French Quarter. The doors were open and a nice breeze was coming in. It was really nice after being in that stinking hole of a cell.

A man dressed in a fancy military dress uniform was sitting at the desk, reading some official-looking papers, when Marti and Mia were escorted into the room. He lifted his head, his gaze sharpening. He looked Mia up and down, kind of slow. A little smile came to his face and he licked his lips. Mia's skin crawled. *Yep, the commandant. Black hair, reptile eyes, narrow mean mouth.* It was him, all right. *Wish I was back in Kansas.*

The commandant stood up and walked leisurely around the desk. He didn't blink. He just stared at Mia and Marti. "Which of you is the whore of Lieutenant Aiden Smith?" His voice was very pleasant, very polite.

Mia didn't answer. *Marti* didn't answer. Mia didn't have to look at her girlfriend to know that Marti was shaking like a leaf. She wasn't doing such a good job of looking cool, either.

The commandant whipped around on Marti. "Is it you?"

Mia resented that. *Of course,* he would think it was Marti. She *was* the prettier one. But Mia still resented it.

Marti's mouth worked. "Wha – wha –?"

The commandant sighed. He shook his head. He clasped his hands behind his back and walked slowly over to the window. He stood silhouetted between the open doors and looked outside. He looked like he had all the time in the world.

Glass panes shattered. The wall on the opposite side of the room spit plaster, followed by the distinct crack of a delayed report.

The commandant staggered back.

The guards standing behind Mia and Marti surged forward.

The commandant fell against the beautiful desk. His eyes and nostrils and mouth were flared wide open. He looked really shocked. But then he straightened up, furiously waving the guards back.

"Oh, missed." Mia didn't realize she had said it out loud until the commandant spit out a vile curse. He strode over to Mia and backhanded her across the face. The heavy ring on his finger cut her face, but Mia didn't notice that right away because she was too busy seeing lights. Mia staggered sideways into one of the guards and he grabbed her, holding her up.

"Ai-ya!"

Mia shook her head free of stars, and she saw the most amazing sight. Her best friend in the whole world was karate kicking the commandant! Marti landed two or three good blows, driving back the commandant, before the guards could grab her shoulders. So she kicked them, too. She even whipped her hands up and backhand bitch-slapped one of them in the face. There was the crack of cartilage and blood spurted from the guard's nose. The guard grunted but he held on to her wriggling shoulders.

"You go, girl!" Mia shouted. Inspired, she stomped down on her guard's toes. He shook her like she was a rat.

Marti couldn't win, of course. It wasn't long before she was subdued. But she wasn't shaking anymore. She was breathing hard, her eyes were shining, and she looked really militant. She blew a blonde curl out of her face.

The commandant walked over to face Marti, but Mia noticed he stayed a respectful distance away from her feet. He didn't look mad anymore. He smiled at her, a truly evil smile. He almost purred. "I will enjoy taming this one."

Broken Nose guard glared at Marti. "Shall we put them back in the cell, commandant?" He cracked his knuckles loudly. Mia didn't like the look on his face.

"No! Put them in my private quarters. I will have something pleasant to look forward to while we are out looking for that shooter!"

Chapter Nine

The guards herded Marti and Mia out of the commandant's office and down another hall. They were roughly pushed into another room and the door was slammed shut and locked. As soon as they were alone, Marti did a couple of hip shimmies. She waved her bound wrists over her head. "Oh yeah! Oh yeah! I kicked some *butt*! Who rocks, huh?"

"You do! I love you, blah-blah-blah. Now help me find something to cut these ties off of our wrists." Mia started prowling around.

Marti pouted. She tossed her blonde hair back over her shoulders. "Spoilsport." But she started snooping around, too.

Mia saw that they weren't in a cell, but instead in a kind of austere bedroom. Curiously, she looked around. There was a wide bed with a wrought iron headboard and footboard and chains. There was a tall wooden T-shaped thingy with chains. There was a sawhorse thingy with chains. There were chains bolted into a wall. Mia was beginning to see a pattern. Whatever else it was, it wasn't a fun-house kind of place. "I've got a really, really bad feeling about this room."

"Uh, Mia? There's some stuff in these drawers."

"Let me guess – chains." Mia was really being sarcastic as she looked around again at the furnishings. Then she turned to see that Marti was standing in front of a long piece of furniture that looked kind of like a squatty dresser. "What's in there? Naughty costumes?"

"Well, no. There are leather whips and paddles and the kind of pliers like we would use to remove some really big splinters. Like, maybe, from a nail gun accident."

Marti and Mia looked at each other.

Mia looked again at the wall with the chains bolted to it. It was a white wall, except for some weird fauxing. Splotches and sprays of an ugly rust color.

Mia's stomach turned over. When she tried to speak, she couldn't make her voice much louder than a whisper. She held up her bound wrists. It didn't surprise her to see that her hands were shaking. "Anything else in there that we can use to cut these ties?"

Marti's eyes were huge. She nodded, quick-bobbing her head up and down. Mia was glad to see that she wasn't the only one who could stand in for a bobble-head toy. Marti gingerly reached into the drawer and lifted out some big clippers. Mia preferred not to think what those were used for. It wasn't for trimming toenails – at least, not in the usual way.

They managed to cut the plastic ties off of their wrists and rubbed the soreness from them while they looked around some more. There was another door in the side of the room but it was also locked. Mia looked at the new door, frowning as she considered it. "Well, even if we get the door open to the corridor that overlooks the courtyard, the guards will see us. I guess we should try to pick the lock on this other door and see where it leads."

Marti agreed. She rummaged in her handbag and came up with her cross stitch needles. "All these locks look ancient. I bet this will work."

Marti knit her brows in concentration and delicately plied the cross stitch needles to the lock. It clicked. Mia high-fived her before they very quietly eased the door open. They looked through the crack at a huge, sumptuous bedroom suite. Mia knew instantly whose suite it had to be and she made a face. "I'll give you two guesses whose bedroom that is."

Marti frowned, looking puzzled. "I've been thinking, Mia. It's really weird, but I keep thinking the lounge-lizard in charge looks familiar."

Mia braced herself. She remembered how well she had taken to the realization she was inside of a movie. And she'd had Aiden beside her. "Uh, Marti? Do you remember the movie we were watching?"

"Well, sure I do! We were grabbed right there in the theater and –" Marti's eyes rounded. "No-no-no! You're not saying – that guy *can't* be the commandant! He's just in a *movie*! He's *not real*!" She looked around, kind of dazed and horrified. Her body folded and she plopped onto the floor on her butt. "I do not *believe* this! I *do not* believe this!"

Mia gently closed the door on the commandant's bedroom. No one was in there at the moment, but she didn't know when a servant or someone else might walk in. Until Marti got over her mild hysterics, Mia thought it would be best to play like the door hadn't been picked open.

Mia kept her voice very mild and non-judgmental. "The first time, I went into major melt-down. You're doing really good!"

Marti glared at her. "I am *fine*! It's just the *shock*." A trembling grin tugged at her lips. "I've always wanted to be in the movies." She giggled and fell back on the floor, waving her arms and legs madly in the air.

Mia looked down at her worriedly. "Marti, you're starting to worry me. You're not going to snap or anything, are you? Because I really don't think I can think of a way to save us if you go wacko on me!"

Marti sat up. Calmly, she climbed to her feet and dusted herself off. She closed her eyes, took a deep breath and pressed her palms together. "Ahm...ahm...ahm..."

"I hate to point this out, but I don't think this is the time to go into a zen state."

"I am *centering* myself."

"Ok, grasshopper. But hurry it up. We need to find a way out of here before torture guy comes back."

Mia's sarcasm kind of snapped Marti back. She gave a decisive nod. "Right. Focus on our priorities. First, escape. Second, deal with craziness. Third, don't follow any mad hatters."

"Do you have an important date?" Mia quipped. Marti shot her a look that should have seared her like fish on a hot grill. Mia grinned at her and made kissy-fish noises. "You love me. You know you do."

"Dork."

"Freak."

They grinned at each other.

Mia felt better. Maybe some of Marti's centering had rubbed off on her. She squeezed her hands together and glanced around the torture chamber. "Okay, let's see if there is anything around here that could be useful."

"Like maybe a phone?"

Mia just looked at her. "Ri-ight. Like a phone."

Mia didn't want to touch anything, so she just did a lot of peering into the corners of the room and around the contraptions with chains. Marti was poking around in the squatty dresser, muttering to herself. When Mia glanced at her, she saw that Marti had her face screwed up, like she smelled something bad.

There was nothing in the fun-house that they could use, except a few knives. Mia thoughtfully took those and tucked them here and there in her clothes. Marti silently watched her, not looking horrified or anything, just watching her. Mia defended herself. "I'm a nurse. I can probably slice and dice if I have to. I'm just saying."

Marti only nodded.

There was a window in the room, but it had metal bars set in it, so that wasn't an escape option.

They opened the door to the bedroom suite. Mia scurried over to the door that would open onto the same corridor that the torture room faced. Slowly, ever so slowly, she pushed an iron bolt into place. That would stop someone from coming in and surprising them.

Marti was still looking for a phone or exit door or anything else that could help them. She disappeared into another room, reemerged. "Bathroom," she whispered.

"I'll check over here." Mia opened another door and then just stood in awe. It was a huge walk-in closet. The commandant was a clothes horse. The man had a serious wardrobe, all fancy uniforms and shiny boots and military hats. There was a big corkboard covered with all kinds and sizes of medals and ribbons. One entire wall was paneled with mirrors. Mia could just imagine him strutting in front of the mirror, admiring his newest uniform and shiniest medals. If he had been a villain with long moustaches, he probably would have twirled them.

Mia shut the door and shook her head. "Just the closet."

"That leaves – " Marti's gaze traveled to the bank of wide windows opening along the outside wall. There was a gorgeous view of sky and ocean and nothing else. Mia didn't like the nothing else part. Marti hurried over and leaned out. When she pulled her head in, she looked excited. "This is our way out!"

Mia joined her. She looked out of the window. *Still just sky and ocean.* She looked down. The wall looked almost sheer and there were rocks and waves crashing far, far below at the bottom. Only a tiny, tiny strip of ground separated the ocean and rocks from the wall. Mia swallowed and backpedaled away from the window. "Nuh-uh. No way, no how."

"Oh, come on, Mia! It's not that bad. Look, it's not much different from the rock wall at home."

"Oh yes, it is." Mia had gone with Marti a few times to the gym and tried the climbing wall with her. Marti was like a lizard on that rock. Mia spent more time dangling in the harness than she did crab-walking from one itty bitty piece to the next. It probably had to do with her center of gravity. She spared a curse for her apple butt. "You are not Thelma and I am not Louise."

Marti took Mia's hand and led her back. She started talking to her in her soothing nurse voice. "Now, now. There's nothing to be afraid of. I'll go first. I'll tell you where to put your hands and your feet. It will be fine, I promise!"

"I can't! I just can't do it, Marti!" Mia looked down but it wasn't at the intimidating wall. She kept seeing a vision of herself, over and over, going splat on those faraway rocks and the waves turning red. She felt kind of sick to her stomach. She whimpered. "Poor Wile E. Coyote! Do you remember the coyote, Marti? Over the cliff, splat! I will never, *ever* laugh at him again!"

"Well, we can't stay here! Creepy mean guy is going to come back! And he likes big pliers!"

Marti had a point. Mia sucked up her meager courage. "Okay, roadrunner. I'll go out the window. Beep-beep."

Marti looked at her kind of funny. "You worry me sometimes, Mia. You really do."

"I worry myself. Especially when I agree to *climb down a cliff with no harness*!" Mia was bleating the last bit because Marti had already swung her legs out of the window and her head was disappearing.

Mia clutched the window sill and watched as her girlfriend started climbing down. Pretty soon, Marti looked up. Marti smiled at her. Her eyes were shining. Mia wondered why she had ever liked her.

"Okay, Mia! Your turn! You saw where I put my feet and hands, didn't you? So *come on*. I'll talk you down. You can *do* it, girl!"

"Rah-rah and pom-poms, too," Mia muttered. But she didn't say it too loud. She was too busy edging herself over the window sill and feeling with her feet. She felt butterflies fluttering low in her belly. It was not a comforting feeling. Then all she could see, just inches in front of her face, was rough stone and rock. Her fingers soon felt like she had used sandpaper on them. She was sweating. It was annoying to have sweat trickling down from her forehead into her eyes and not being able to wipe it away. The whole time, she could hear Marti's cheerful voice. Mia was so glad that she never shut up.

The waves sounded louder. Every time Mia heard them crashing on the rocks, she flinched, but she didn't look down. She just behaved like a good crab and inched her way sideways and down and zigged and zagged some more.

"Okay, Mia! I'm down now. Just a little farther. Put your foot to the left. That's it. Just a little far – "

"Oh, thank you God." Mia concentrated on the last few holds. Then her reaching, searching foot touched terra firma. "Yes, yes, yes!" She let go of the hated rock wall, gave it a one-fingered salute and spun around, grinning like a fool.

Mia's face kind of froze.

Marti was standing with her hands raised up above her head. There were two men, one pointing a rifle at Marti and the other one pointing a rifle at her. *Well, howdy-do-de.* Mia groaned in exasperation. "I am so darn tired of looking down the wrong end of a projectile tube!"

"You will come with us."

Mia planted her hands on her hips and tried to brazen it out. *It's a movie. Nobody really dies.* "Or what? You're going to shoot us?" She heard a moan come from Marti's direction. Suddenly, Mia wasn't so confident. *Okay, wait. If we're inside the movie, then maybe we can die.* The logic was twisted, but, unfortunately, sound.

Mia stared at the man.

The man grinned. He didn't have all of his teeth. His nose looked like it had been broken more than once. He was not a handsome fellow. He cocked the gun. Mia could hear the cold metallic click over the crash of the waves.

"Oh. Okay. Since you put it that way."

Marti and Mia were hustled down to the low-rising rocks. Spray misted over them and Mia could practically feel her hair frizzing up. She scowled. *Bad hair is absolutely the last straw.* There was a tiny strip of beach where there was a beached rowboat. The unexpected escort forced the two women at gunpoint to sit in the boat. Then one of the men took the oars and the other sat in the prow of the boat with his gun pointing at the captives.

Mia didn't like the way the gun barrel shifted every time the boat bounced over a wave. It was kind of like watching a cobra's weaving head. *Very, very dangerous.* She cleared her throat. "You're not the commandant's men?"

Both of the men hawked and spit into the surging saltwater.

"Guess not. So! Where are we going? Pretty how the sun sparkles on the water. Are we going to be crab meat?" Mia felt the hard jab of an elbow in her ribs. She looked at Marti. "*What*!"

Marti glared at her. "Just shut up, Mia! Shut up!"

"We take you to Cadero."

Mia sighed. "Oh, this will be fun."

The boat trip wasn't that long, just a short row across the narrow neck of a sea channel. The man rowed the boat so close to the beach that the boat bottom scraped on sand. The man in the prow motioned his gun at the women. "You will get out now!"

Marti looked over the side of the boat. Her brows snapped together. "There's still ocean out there." She pointed down at her little black slip-ons. "These are expensive leather!"

The man in the prow cocked his gun. It sounded very loud over the lazy slap of water against the boat.

Mia plastered a smile on her face. She waved in a friendly way at the gunman, while she whispered fiercely out of the corner of her mouth. "Uh, Marti – *gun?*"

Marti sniffed. She slipped off her shoes and carefully put them into her huge handbag. Adjusting the handbag so that was lying across her back, she swung over the side of the boat with graceful ease, splashing feet first into the shallow waves.

Mia clambered over the side, grunting, and jumped awkwardly into the water. It was only about calf high, so she didn't think there would be any sharks. She waded to shore, following her girlfriend. Mia was wearing tennies, so she hadn't bothered removing them. It was hot enough that her shoes would steam dry.

One of the men pulled the boat up onto the beach. The other one paced beside the two women, his gun angled towards them. Mia and Marti didn't run and not just because of the armed men. There was simply nowhere to go. There was just a big jumble of rocks jutting straight up out of the white sand.

The nearest man grunted at them and motioned with his gun at the rocks. "We go up."

Mia sighed. "Why am I not surprised?" She looked at Marti and crossed her eyes. "Do I *look* like a mountain goat?"

Marti giggled. "No, silly! You don't have a goatee!"

Both men hawked and spit and glared.

"I don't think they appreciate our humor."

Marti shrugged. "I don't care what they think." She put her shoes back on.

One of the men climbed up the rocks. Mia and Marti followed. The other man closed up behind them. Mia hoped the gun he was holding didn't go off accidentally. It had to be pointed right at her butt.

They climbed for what seemed a long time. Marti just kept moving ahead, never faltering, but Mia had to push herself to keep up. Panting, Mia glared at Marti's slim back. "Unfair! You've always been freakily athletic."

Marti glanced down over her shoulder, grinning. "Come on, Mia! Keep up!"

By the time they topped out and began seeing some grass and trees mixed in with the rocky hillside, Mia's calf muscles were burning. The air was hot and humid and sticky. She paused to wipe the sweat out of her eyes.

The man behind her didn't like her to stop. He grunted, motioning with the gun. Mia tried to buy a little more breathing time. "We're lost, aren't we?"

He looked insulted. "Of course we are not lost! Go!" He jerked the gun again.

Mia sighed, slapped at an insect buzzing her arm, and plodded onward.

Before long, it looked like to her that they were following some kind of animal track. She couldn't see the turquoise water anymore, just more and more rock and spiky grass. Then the man in the lead ducked under some more rocks and disappeared from sight. Marti and Mia obediently followed him. The bright sun abruptly vanished and Mia realized that they were inside a cave.

Mia's eyes adjusted to the gloom and she could see there were several men already in the cave. Some were squatting around the flickering yellow flames of a small fire. Others were lying on blankets. A lot of guns and knives were scattered around. Mia could smell smoke and dank stone and something else.

"Phew!" Marti waved her hands in front of her face, wrinkling her nose. Mia's own nostrils quivered. The guys didn't have a nice flush toilet.

Every head turned toward the women. Hard, unfriendly eyes stared at them. Mia didn't feel too comfortable. She didn't think Marti did, either, because Marti crossed her arms and rubbed her hands up and down them.

A big man got up from where he was sitting on a boulder and walked towards them with the fluid grace of a panther. He said a few words. While one of the armed men stayed by Mia and Marti, the other started talking in a low voice, gesturing at the two women. The big man studied Mia and Marti like they were stink bugs.

Mia instantly recognized him from the action movie.

Cadero looked like a mercenary. Big, tough, a mean, lean machine. His black eyes were cold. He sported a jagged scar down one side of his face that stood out against his brown skin. His long black hair was tied back with a leather thong. He was pretty darn good-looking in a dangerous macho way.

Mia heard Marti let out a tiny sigh. She knew exactly what Marti was thinking. Marti had always liked the beefed-up Latin types.

"Rambo at one o'clock," Mia muttered.

"Oh yeah."

Cadero overheard her. He thrust the guard back with one hand splayed on the man's chest. A fanatic light had leapt into his eyes. "You know John Rambo?" It was like he shot the question at her out of a pistol.

"No, but I know all about his legend." Mia shot right back at him. "Have you ever heard of Sylvester Stallone?"

Marti squeaked. "Mia!"

Cadero looked confused. "Who is Sylvester Stallone?"

"Sly Stallone and John Rambo are close. Very, very close." Mia thought about it and smiled. "Closer than brothers. He's the man behind Rambo."

Cadero looked intrigued. "Do you know Stallone? I would like to know this man who is, as you say, closer than a brother to John Rambo."

Mia sighed. Sometimes it was hard to remember where she was. She shook her head. "No, I've just read about him."

He considered what she had said, then shook his head with disapproval. "This Sylvester Stallone should not jeopardize his connections. He should keep a lower profile. What does he do?"

Mia debated how to tweek the truth. "Sly is like Rambo's money man."

He looked impressed. "Ah, then it is comprehensible. Everyone needs a financier."

Mia grinned, starting to enjoy herself in a jerky way. "Sly Stallone is really close to Rocky Balboa, too."

"The fighter! Yes, yes! This Sly Stallone, he chooses good men!"

"Quit already, Mia!" Marti glared at her.

Mia couldn't help it. She laughed. She pointed at Marti. "And she is one kickass mama. She kicked the commandant's butt!"

Cadero's gaze swung away from Mia and zeroed in on her best friend. His stare was intent and hot and assessing. Marti blushed. She said modestly, "Well, I did get in a few good hits. And I broke one of the guards' noses."

"What is this? A guard, too?"

Mia could tell that Cadero was impressed. She thought that could only be a good thing. "The guards outnumbered Marti, three to one. *And* her hands were tied."

"Madre dios!" Cadero took a step towards her, looking down at Marti as if she was spun of pure gold. "Such fire! Such courage!"

Marti pouted her lower lip. Her eyelashes fluttered. She looked adorable. "The commandant shouldn't have hit my friend in the face." Her voice was all breathy.

Cadero leaned over her. He raised one hand to gently cup her face. "You are truly a prize, mi linda."

Marti giggled.

Mia noticed that no one was expressing worry about her sore, bloodied face. Mia pouted a little herself. Not that anyone noticed. "The commandant thought so, too. He said that he would enjoy taming Marti. That's why we climbed down the wall. We didn't like the looks of his little fun-house torture chamber."

Cadero jerked around. His black eyes blazed. He snarled. "I will kill him twice over! Once for my sister! And again, because he dared to voice such sacrilege!" He waved his hand, as though he had just remembered. "Oh, and also because I am the leader of the revolution."

"Yeah?" Mia glanced around at the motley crew in the cave. The raggedly dressed men, even if they were armed, didn't look like much of a revolution. "It looks like you need some help. I know just the man."

His whole face lit up. "John Rambo?"

"No; Aiden Smith."

Chapter Ten

It took awhile for Cadero to get over his disappointment that he wasn't going to get Rambo's help, but he grudgingly agreed that Special Ops was a good second-best. He grimaced, making his scar twist in a grotesque way. "I do not trust outsiders, you understand. But perhaps, we can help each other."

He issued orders that a secret message was to be taken to the cantina. The bartender would relay it through channels to Aiden, so that a meeting could be set up. He pointed at Mia, then jerked his thumb at a man who stood nearby. "You will go with my man. You will be hidden above the cantina. When this Lieutenant Aiden Smith comes, then he will believe what you tell him about me and my men."

Mia nodded happily. She was going to get out of the stinking cave and see Aiden again. She couldn't wait. "Okay! Come on, Marti. Let's get going."

Cadero showed his very white teeth. His black eyes gleamed. "Your chica remains with me. I must have insurance. Perhaps I shall take her to my sister."

Marti's eyes rounded. She looked up real quick into Cadero's face, then dropped her gaze. She circled one toe of her expensive leather slip-on in the dirt of the cave.

"Uh, you mind if I talk to my *chica* privately?" Mia smiled politely. Good manners couldn't hurt anything.

Cadero waved his hand. "But of course not! It is natural that you will wish to say goodbye."

Mia didn't like the sound of that. Cadero walked away and so did the guard. Darting a wary gaze around, Mia grabbed Marti's arm. She hissed at her, real low. "I can't leave you here! You've got to sneak out or – or something!"

"I can't. You heard him. He wants me for insurance."

Marti didn't look frightened. Mia couldn't figure it out. She shook her girlfriend's arm. "Marti! What if something bad happens? I-I might never see you again."

Marti got a small grin on her face. "Mia, it's going to be *all right*. He's going to take me to his *sister*, remember?"

Mia stared at her, frowning. "Yeah, so?"

Marti shook her head, like Mia was really dense. "He's taking me to meet his *family*, Mia! Get it? He *likes* me."

"So – you're okay with me going off by myself." Mia was feeling kind of hurt.

"Well, of *course* not, silly! Something bad might happen to *you*! But I just *know* everything is going to be all right." Marti gave her a hug. It made Mia feel a little better.

The guide came back to fetch Mia. "It is time to go." He jerked his head towards the cave entrance. Mia followed him.

At the cave's entrance, Mia hesitated and looked back. Marti waved at her, looking cheerful. Mia waved back and ducked out of the cave. The guide led her away into the rocks and spiky grass. When Mia glanced back again, she couldn't even see where the entrance to the cave was anymore.

The trek was long, dry, and hot. At last, Mia could see the colorful crowded buildings of the town. The church bell tower rose above the tallest flat roofs. The commandant's fortress-like compound hulked above everything else.

Getting unobserved into the town was not that hard. Mia's guide just slapped a floppy native hat over her head and a big woolly blanket thing over her shoulders that hung down to her knees and hid her clothes. Mia felt kind of hot. *Not* that kind of hot, but sweaty, sweat trickling down the back *hot*. Her face felt prickly, despite the shade of the hat. Under the blanket, her clothes clung to her sticky skin.

Armed soldiers in trucks rumbled through the narrow dusty streets. When the trucks roared past, the townspeople and chickens and dogs had to scatter out of the way. The yelling and clucking and yelping mixed with the curses that were shouted after the soldiers. Some of the people shook their fists. But no one paid any attention to Mia or her guide. She just plodded along, watching the dust puff up under her plodding feet. Mia wasn't really thinking about a whole lot, but her mind did seem to be stuck in a rut. *Ice-cold Coke. Iced tea. Frozen margarita.*

At the cantina, Mia was led upstairs and pushed into a tiny airless room under the roof beams. The man muttered for her to keep the shutters closed over the windows. Then he left her there alone and shut the door. It was pretty dim in there, just fingers of sunlight coming in through the uneven wooden shutters.

Mia sat down on the narrow bed. The heat was really bad. She dragged off the hat and the blanket thing. That helped, but not by much. Mia decided it might be cooler if she sat on the floor. *Everyone knows heat rises.* She was just as hot and her butt went to sleep on the hard boards.

Mia didn't know how long she waited. She wasn't really worried or anything. She vaguely suspected the heat kind of put her into a stupor, so she had no worries at all. Her head started to pound. She closed her eyes and drowsed.

Then the door opened and a big figure slipped into the room. Mia scrambled unsteadily to her feet, ready to defend her virtue. Her head swam and she staggered. "Oh, crap."

Large hands grabbed hold of her shoulders. "Mia!"

Mia's head lolled back and she blinked, very slowly. Aiden's face swam into sight. Mia giggled in relief. "Oh, it's you!"

He shook her gently. His deep voice was all rumbly and concerned. "What's wrong with you?"

"I'm just so hot."

He lowered her down to sit on the bed. Next thing Mia knew, a canteen was tilted to her lips and she was greedily drinking tepid metallic water. Mia had never tasted anything so good in her life. Mia perked right up. She tilted her head so she could smile at Aiden. "Hi there, lover boy."

He grasped her chin, lifting her face more towards the murky light. "What happened to your face?"

"The commandant hit me." Mia pouted. This time it worked.

Aiden's face went tight and he barely breathed. *"I'll kill him."*

It was very satisfying on some visceral, primitive level. Mia waved her hand like it was not a big deal. *Brave, brave me.* She felt very British, for some reason. *Keep a stiff upper lip, lads.* "It's nothing. Really, I'm fine."

Aiden stared at her, his brows gradually lowering in a gold bar over his glacial eyes. Annoyance colored his response "That's just like you, Mia."

"Excuse me?" Mia narrowed her eyes at him. She did *not* like his tone of voice.

"You came back for me. You risk yourself to get me back to my team. You somehow manage to get kidnapped by a madman. You blow it off that he hits you!"

Aiden's face was turning red. Mia couldn't believe it. He was being so unreasonable. He obviously knew he couldn't yell because they might be overheard by unwelcome parties, so he was spitting out hissed whispers. Brave Mia morphed into thoroughly pissed Mia. She glared at him. "You *like* it that I'm brave! You said so!"

"I changed my mind!"

Mia squealed in outrage, kind of like Doris Day in a lady-like snit. Being in a movie was growing on her. Her inner drama queen was coming out.

Mia slugged him on the chest. He didn't even blink.

Aiden showed his teeth in a shark grin.

Mia's lips trembled. A lone tear welled and leaked out of one of her eyes. She guessed she didn't have enough liquid in her to squeeze out two tears, but it didn't matter.

Aiden groaned. He swept his arms around her and pulled her close. His breath was warm in her hair. "God, Mia, I can't stand it that you've been in danger."

"Oh, Aiden!" Mia clutched him. "Kiss me quick! And then let's go rescue Marti, okay?"

His warm, firm lips settled on hers. For several glorious, technicolor moments, they sucked face like champs. Mia moaned in her throat. She had missed him so much!

Aiden must have missed her, too. His hands were suddenly everywhere on her. Next thing Mia knew, her jeans and panties were down and Aiden was lifting her up against the white plastered wall. His long calloused fingers bit into her butt cheeks. He thrust up into her quivering center, his big hot boner sliding deliciously home. He growled low in his throat. "*Mia!*"

Mia hissed in her breath. She looped her arms behind his neck and locked her legs around his lean waist. "*Hard,* Aiden!"

His wild bucking set yellow sparks off behind her eyeballs. Mia wound her arms in a strangle-hold around his brawny neck, holding on tight for the ride. Aiden's hard hammering nailed her to the wall. He was grunting like a demented bear. It was quick and dirty and good.

Afterwards, all Aiden had to do was zip himself back up. Mia took a little longer to put herself back together. When she was ready, he pulled her close for a firm, possessive kiss. He nuzzled her neck, his breath sending renewed shivers down her spine. "What's this about Marti?"

"Oh, yeah! I forgot, my bad." Mia told him about her best friend and Cadero and the revolution.

Aiden smiled. His electric blue eyes glinted at her. "You never stop surprising me, Mia. You've saved me days of trying to pull together hard intel. Let's go see about setting up a meeting with Cadero."

When they snuck down the back stairs of the cantina, Aiden and Mia walked right into a trap. There were soldiers everywhere with guns. Fortunately, the bartender and a few others were on Mia and Aiden's side. They had guns, too. Mia kind of hunkered down against the wall, her hands over her ears, while the bullets whizzed everywhere. After awhile, the soldiers all fell dead to the floor. The acrid smoke was still eddying in the air when Aiden casually turned around to talk to the bartender.

That's when Mia saw the soldier who was hiding behind a big potted palm. She realized that he had the drop on Aiden. His lips were pulled back in an evil smile.

Mia leaped to her feet and yelled a warning. Aiden whipped around. Mia's heart stopped. Almost as though time had frozen, she saw what was going to happen. Aiden wasn't going to be able to beat the soldier to the draw.

It was an action movie, so Mia had to take action. Her man was in harm's way. Quick as a flash, Mia pulled a knife out of her sleeve and threw it. The knife turned end over end in slow motion. Then the point struck the soldier in the throat. He threw up his hands, gurgled, and fell to the ground.

Mia grinned. "I love how things work out at the movies."

Aiden was open-mouthed. He looked at the dead soldier, then at Mia. She shrugged, like she threw knives at bad guys every day. She tossed her head. "I got skills." He grinned.

Then everyone got down to business. The bartender told Aiden where to meet Cadero. Someone slapped a big floppy hat and a blanket thingy over Mia, to her disgust. "Did somebody go upstairs to get these things when I wasn't looking?"

No one answered her. Everyone was too busy getting rid of dead soldiers.

Then they were off, following one of the men from the bar. He seemed to be a nervous, overly cautious man. He led them in circles, all over town, edging around corners and slinking over rooftops. Mia thought it was really kind of neat. Now she knew what it was like to be inside a cat's head.

Aiden and Mia ended up in a deserted alley, standing under a broken arch. Cadero was waiting. He wasn't wearing a floppy hat and blanket thingy. *Lucky him.* Mia took her hat off and fanned her hot face with it.

"Aiden Smith? I am Cadero." He said his name with a lot of pride and stuck out his impressive chest. With narrowed eyes, he looked Aiden up and down. His big scarred hand was resting on the big gun holstered at his hip.

"I understand you're the leader of the revolution." Aiden looked him over, too. His big hand was curved over the top of the big gun hanging from a strap over his shoulder.

The testosterone was so thick in the air that Mia sneezed. They both looked at her. They both frowned. "Sorry. Just get on with it, okay? We haven't got a whole lot of time." Mia was thinking that more than half of the movie had to be over already and they hadn't blown anything up yet. Mia didn't want the audience to get bored.

"The woman is right." Cadero flashed a smile, but his black eyes were cold. "We are to be comrades in arms, yes?"

Aiden smiled. It wasn't the sexy grin that he always flashed for Mia. He looked dangerous instead. His electric blue eyes were very bright and hard. "All right. Let's make our plans."

Mia stood around, kind of bored, while they hashed things out. Then they were shaking hands and grunting their goodbyes. Mia quickly looked from one to the other. She threw up her hands. "Hold it! Hold everything! What about my friend? I want her back, like now!"

Cadero flashed another glimpse of very white teeth. "Your chica is safe, do not fear. She will stay with me for a little while longer." He turned and walked away, his man falling into place behind him.

"But that wasn't the deal!" Mia was furious. Cadero didn't turn around and she couldn't go after him because Aiden was holding her back. He had a hand wrapped around one of her upper arms and his tight fingers rubbed the scratchy blanket thingy unpleasantly against her skin. "Let go of me! *Come back here!*"

"Mia, this isn't the way to help your friend. It isn't safe to stay here. Come on, we've got to get back to headquarters!" Aiden began hauling her back down the crooked alley the way they had come. He was walking fast. It was hard for Mia to keep from stumbling. Not because he was striding so quickly, but because he was moving her along with him when she didn't want to move.

"But what about Marti?" Mia tried digging her heels into the cracked pavement, but she couldn't get much traction. She wasn't doing anything to slow them down, let alone braking.

Finally, Aiden stopped. He pulled her into the shelter of a deep-seated doorway. Letting go of her arm, he laid his hands on her shoulders and squeezed. The look on his face was real serious. "I will see that Marti is gotten back safely. Do you trust me?"

Mia looked up into his baby blues, seeing the sincerity reflected there. Reluctantly, she nodded. "Okay. But if you screw this up, Aiden, you won't screw me!"

Aiden gaped, his jaw sagging. His hold slackened and Mia twisted free. She stomped up the alley, but not before she saw the utter shock of comprehension on his face.

Mia grinned, evilly, and slapped the stupid floppy hat back on her head. Instantly, heat encased her head, but she knew she could handle it. She had just thrown down a major power play and won. *A guy can always be motivated by sex, right?*

She heard Aiden's heavy boot steps slapping up behind her. *"Mia!"*

"Talk to the hand, Aiden!"

Mia didn't turn around, but speeded up. She decided Marti was going to be all right. Her hunky action hero would see to it! She rounded a corner of the twisted alley.

"You there! Chico!"

Mia faltered, nearly tripping on her own feet. She whipped her head, feeling hot breeze under the brim of her awful hat as it smacked her forehead. She saw a uniformed soldier planted wide-legged several feet in front of her. He seemed to be staring straight at her. Her heart started pit-a-patting at a rapid rate. She swallowed and froze in place. She quickly looked to both sides, hoping she wasn't the one being singled out, but unfortunately there wasn't anyone else there. Just the empty, twisted alley between solid walls of buildings. She seemed to hear the single raucous cry of a happy vulture.

"Yes – you!" The soldier pointed at her. He had a pistol out. Luckily *it* wasn't pointed at her. "Chico!"

Mia was glad that her awful disguise at least made him take her for a boy.

The soldier was standing in the mouth of the narrow alley. Behind him, on the wider street, a troop truck lumbered slowly by. "Have you seen a big man pass this way?"

Mia didn't dare look beyond her shoulder. Out of the corner of her eye, she saw a blur of motion. She guessed that Aiden had jumped into hiding in one of the deep doorways. But if the soldier decided to come closer, he would be able to see that part of the alley. Mia felt the sick drumming of her pulse in her ears. She shook her head vigorously.

The soldier wore star-quality wrap-around black sunglasses. The sunlight glinted off the silver rims. He half-raised the pistol. "Are you sure, chico? A big man with a scar on his face?"

She shook her head again, but more slowly. She shrugged, making the heavy woolly blanket thingy sway around her dirty blue-jeaned legs. Nervously, she scuffed at the dirt on the pavement. Under cover of the blanket thingy, she slid a couple of her knives free from their places in her sleeves. She carefully angled her arms so that she could sweep her hands out past the heavy covering. Sweat made ponds of her armpits. Huge drops trickled down her spine, down the backs of her legs.

Her brain was screaming at her. *Idiot! Bullets travel faster than knives! Do real people die in the movies – inquiring minds want to know!*

The soldier snorted his disgust. He lowered the pistol. "Imbecile!" He turned around and stomped off out of sight. Dust motes danced in the sun where he had been.

Mia stumbled to the nearest cracked plastered wall and sagged against it. She breathed really fast through her nose. She felt like she might possibly want to throw up. She was still gripping tight the hard hilts of the knives. The whole world appeared to be far, far away and she blinked owlishly at it through a shocked haze. *I could be dead right now! Aiden could be dead!*

Through the blood pounding in her head, she heard a low penetrating whistle. Mia straightened and stumbled a few steps back the way she had come.

A large hand fisted in the blanket thingy, whirled her around, and jerked her nearly off her feet. Mia fell forward against a broad familiar chest. She smelled sweaty male musk. She burrowed against him, sweeping her fists around him.

He flinched. *"Ow!"*

She had forgotten the knives in her hands. She eased back from him. She still felt kind of disconnected, so she was only mildly concerned. "Oh, sorry! Did I hurt you?"

Aiden glared down at her. He reached behind himself, gingerly feeling around on his back. "You did that on purpose!"

"If I'd done it on purpose, I'd have done this!" Mia stepped in close and angled one of the knives suggestively high up between his brawny thighs. The point pricked fabric. She literally felt his entire body stiffen. He didn't twitch a muscle. She didn't think he even breathed.

"Uh – Mia? Sweetheart?"

The world came back in a rush. Mia felt a really heady sense of power. It was a very interesting sensation. It drove away all of the nausea. Mia relished it. Suddenly, she felt much better. "Don't worry! I like it too much where it is!" She stepped back and serenely smiled up at him from under the brim of the battered hat.

"*Shit!*" Aiden breathed through his nose. His eyes were blazing blue flame. He looked like he was going to say something hasty, but then apparently thought better about it. He shifted the big gun slung from his shoulder into his hands. "Is the soldier gone?"

Mia nodded. She felt a new hit of anxiety. "But I think we should get out of here fast, Aiden! I caught a glimpse of a truck with armed troops. They're looking for Cadero, but I don't think they'd mind finding you!"

"I think you're right. Let's go!" Aiden started walking. Mia kept pace with him. He glanced down warily. "And put those knives away! Don't you know it's dangerous to play with sharp objects?"

Mia rolled her eyes. She hiccoughed on a hysterical giggle. "Oh, all right!"

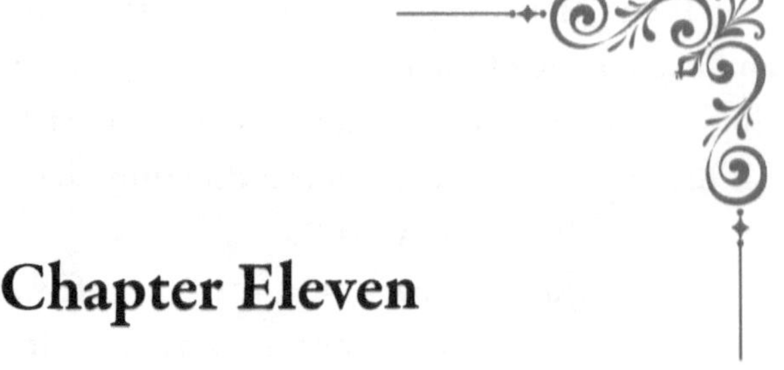

Chapter Eleven

When Aiden and Mia got back to headquarters, the first thing Mia did was trash the hated floppy hat and wooly blanket cover thingy in a big metal can. It had been the worst disguise ever designed. She never wanted to see it again. The next thing she wanted was an ice-cold soda. She didn't have any money, so she vigorously kicked the machine until it delivered. She greedily sucked soda down, like a frat boy sucking a keg dry, and wiped her mouth. She crunched the can on her forehead, just because in movie land she could, and tossed it for a three-pointer.

She was pleased. Apparently, she had all kinds of unrealized talents.

Aiden had watched her performance. He shook his head and sighed in a put-upon way. "Mia, stop showing off."

Mia stuck out her tongue. Then she grinned at him. "You're just jealous because I'm more macho than you are!"

Aiden quirked his brows. Laughter gleamed in his electric blue eyes. He flexed his bulging biceps, but didn't say anything. Mia scowled at him. He was gorgeous. His uniform was a little dusty, but he wasn't rumpled and streaked with sweat and dirt like she was.

Mia knew she looked a fright. She thoughtfully scratched an insect bite on her arm as she shot a longing glance towards the exit. She really wanted a shower, being all sticky and sweaty and fragrant. But she and Aiden had been ordered to go directly in to see the general.

Mia pouted. She was a civilian. She had shower rights.

Aiden hadn't missed that glance of hers. He eyed her sternly. "Come quietly or I will put a strong-hold on you, sweetheart."

Mia grumbled but she went.

The general was waiting for them. He glanced at Mia's streaked, dirty appearance, but he didn't comment. Instead, he stared fiercely at her, his hands clasped behind his back. He rolled his unlit cigar between his teeth. "I want you to recount every detail of your capture and escape, Dr. Haven. Any detail could be of vital importance."

"Yes, sir." Mia resigned herself. *Report first. Shower second.* She decided to omit that she and Marti had been snatched out of a theater by on-screen goons. But she told the general everything else that she could remember.

When she told about the dramatic meeting with the commandant, she ignored Aiden's low growl. He muttered a nasty curse when she described the fun-house torture room. She just kept pulling stuff out of her memory for the general. He asked questions here and there, which triggered more details that she hadn't even realized she knew. She even told the general about counting the doors in the cell block corridor.

The general's bushy eyebrows twitched upwards. His hard eyes warmed with a gleam of approval. "Very good, Dr. Haven! That's solid information we didn't have."

It didn't take long for her to tell everything she knew about the cave and Cadero's men, but the general grilled her for more details – like how many men had she seen and what kind of weapons were they armed with and could she find the cave again? He seemed a little disappointed that she couldn't do better with her answers. At last, Mia just spread her hands helplessly. "I'm sorry, general. That's as good as it gets."

"All in all, you've done very well, Dr. Haven." Then the general turned to Aiden. He bared his big teeth around his cigar, his expectation obvious. "All right, Smith! Tell me about this Cadero."

While Aiden made his report, Mia took out of one of knives hidden under her sleeves and played with it. She caught a few odd glances tossed her way from the uniformed personnel, but she ignored them. Mia grinned to herself. A kickass mama, who could take down a bad guy with a knife thrown at the throat, didn't care about the opinions of others. She was an action movie goddess! She could make or break her own rules. *I rock!*

She sighed. She let her inner bravado sag into disgruntlement. *I stink and want a shower!*

The general barked a few more questions, but she could see that he was pleased with Aiden's report. He was smiling and rolling his cigar around between his teeth. "Well done! The attack will commence at 0500 tomorrow."

For several minutes, Mia had been thinking hard, and not just about warm water and soap bubbles. She spoke up even though she felt a little sick to her stomach. Her thoughts hadn't been Happy-Meals. "General, I'd like an extra word with you."

The general turned to her. She easily detected the impatience shading his expression. He was an important busy man with important business to take care of, after all. However, he was polite. "Yes, Dr. Haven? What is it?"

"I volunteer myself as the medic for this mission." Mia saw the surprise on the general's face and she straightened her shoulders. Mia discreetly slipped the knife back up her sleeve. She didn't think it looked professional to be toying with it, not when she was making a serious pitch. "I am experienced at triage, probably better than anyone you have on the hospital staff."

"No!" Aiden's bellow was explosive. He started forward. "General, sir!"

The general waved Aiden back. The general's fierce old eyes, cold and speculative, locked squarely on Mia. "While I applaud your dedication, you're a civilian, Dr. Haven."

"Yes, sir, but I am a civilian who is known to Cadero and also to your people. I feel that I am uniquely qualified, sir." Mia could feel her heart beating fast. She wanted the general to say yes so badly. She didn't look directly at Aiden, but she could see him out of the corner of her eye. He didn't appear happy. Correction – he looked furious.

The general nodded thoughtfully. "You have made some valid points, Dr. Haven. In addition, as you are temporarily attached to the base field hospital, it will not disrupt the regular hospital staff routine to move you into the slot." He rolled his cigar between his teeth. "Very well, Dr. Haven! You will be the acting field medic on this mission. Smith, dismissed!"

"Thank you, sir." Mia smiled gratefully at the general.

"Thank you, general, sir!" It didn't sound like Aiden was grateful.

While Aiden was still saluting, Mia turned on her heel and started walking quickly away. But she wasn't quick enough. She heard rapid footsteps overtaking her. Then she felt a large hand circle around her upper arm and tightly grip it. She was jerked to a stop.

Mia looked up, ready to blast Aiden. But whatever she was going to say shriveled under the fiery glare he leveled on her. Mia thought she actually heard his teeth grinding together as he growled at her. "We're going somewhere we can *talk*, Mia."

Before Mia could think of any really good excuse to avoid 'the talk', they had walked all the way to Aiden's quarters. As soon as they were inside, Aiden pulled Mia around, grabbed her shoulders and shook her. *"What the hell are you thinking, Mia?"*

Mia twisted loose. She snarled back at him. *"Do not* manhandle me! I'm armed and I'm cranky and I know how to hurt you!"

Aiden threw his hands up into the air. He looked wild-eyed. *"Mia!* This isn't a walk in the park that we're talking about! This is a hazardous mission! A dangerous operation! A perilous task! You could be hurt! You might even be killed! Have you even thought about that?"

"Yes, I have! And ditto for you!"

He looked blank. "Well, yeah! But – but doing a mission – that's my job!"

"And it's *my* job to see that you don't bleed out while you're doing *your* job!" Mia folded her arms over her chest. She saw his gaze drop to the plumping movement of her breasts. She was outraged. "Aiden! Stop staring at my bosoms! We're having a disagreement, remember?"

Aiden's gaze shot back up to her face. His cheekbones flushed. "I know what we're doing! I won't allow you to put yourself in jeopardy, Mia! That's my final word!"

Mia stared at him. *He did not just say that. He did not just go Neanderthal!* She realized her jaw had dropped and she snapped it back up. "You won't *allow* me? Is that what you said, soldier-boy?" She advanced on him and poked a finger into his chest. He didn't even wince, of course. "You won't *allow me?* Since when do I have to ask your permission for anything? I'm a grown woman. I've been making my own decisions. I've been taking care of myself for a long time!"

"Taking care of you is my job now," he said quietly. His electric blue eyes were heated with certainty; but he was frowning at her, like he knew he was missing something.

Mia shook her head. She could see that he didn't get it. She felt herself starting to shake inside. "No, Aiden, it isn't. Not if you think you're going to dictate to me. Not if you think you're the only one who has a right to make decisions." Her throat was closing up and she barely got out the last part. *"Not if you think I'm just a freaking job!"*

He looked shocked. "Mia! I don't think of you like that!" He reached out for her.

Mia batted away his hands. She quickly stepped back, out of his reach. "No, Aiden! This can't be fixed with a rub and a tickle."

She backed up some more. He looked confused and worried. He eyed the increased distance between them, then looked at her face. "Uh – Mia?"

"I'm going to bed! Alone!" Mia spun and ran into the bedroom and slammed shut the door. Her chest hurt and her eyes ached from unshed tears. She covered her face with her trembling hands.

Mia bent over, gasping for breath. What had she just done? *The Breakup. Le Divorce. Phantom of the Opera.* Cold slid down her spine. She was suddenly very, very afraid. Action flicks had happy endings. Chick flicks didn't. She was a chick and her flick had flopped big-time.

She half-wished Aiden would come barreling through the door. She straightened. She waited, standing still in the middle of the bedroom, watching the door. But it didn't open. She heard quiet, rustling sounds, then some creaking. She realized what she was hearing was a heavy weight settling onto the sofa.

Aiden wasn't going to follow her. He was going to sleep on the sofa.

Listlessly, Mia pulled off her clothes and dragged herself to the shower. Under the hot spray of water, the dirt ran down the drain, but the black cloud hanging over her didn't. She toweled off and crawled into the bed. After she lay down, she pulled Aiden's pillow into her arms. Mia buried her face in it. She could smell his masculine, musky scent on the pillowcase.

She cried herself to sleep.

AIDEN LAY ON THE HARD sofa, his muscular forearms crossed under his head. Scowling, he stared up into the dark at the ceiling. He couldn't wrap his head around what had just happened. What *did* happen? He and Mia were talking – all of a sudden, she had blown up!

He had a right to be upset. She shouldn't have volunteered for the mission. He brushed aside the established fact of her bravery and her medical qualifications. He knew all that. He just couldn't endure the thought of her being in danger. He wanted her to be safe, that's all. How could that be wrong? *But Mia is Mia. I can't hold her back. I don't want her to change!*

He heard the shower go on, then when it shut off. A few minutes later, he heard a whimpering, sobbing kind of sound. The hairs stood up on the nape of his neck. He jerked up from the sofa, ramming his bare feet to the floor. Then he just sat there, making helpless fists out of his hands on his tight, bunched thighs.

He couldn't go to her.

Aiden set his elbows on his knees and dropped his head, running his hands over his short hair. She had made it clear. She didn't want him. *It's killing me.*

He heaved a huge sigh. Slowly he rotated his body, easing back down flat on the sofa, and settled his legs on the stiff cushions. Hundreds of memories of Mia, and of being with her, flashed one after the other through his mind.

Aiden smiled to himself. His friend Caesar had gotten it wrong. Whatever time he and Mia had together, whether their relationship went on or it ended now, it had all been worth it. *No matter what happens, I don't regret one minute!*

And suddenly, he realized something. Mia had been trying to tell him that they were equal partners. They shared safe times and they shared dangerous times. Nothing mattered except that they shared them together. *That doesn't mean I'm not still mad at her for volunteering for this mission!*

Mia had been marked. She was too well known to the enemy. That was what was bothering him so much. Even as a medic, she would be a prime target.

Usually he slept like a baby before a mission. He didn't think he'd get much sleep that night. The eddying air was cool against his nude body. He wished he was wrapped around his warm woman.

THE DULL ROAR OF THE helicopter enclosed them all. The troops sat on the hard benches on either side of the airship. They had black camo streaked over their faces, they had guns, and they were all waiting to jump into battle.

Mia was deathly afraid. Adrenaline buzzed through her. One of her knees was jumping up and down all by itself.

Over the noise of the helicopter, Aiden shouted into his comm. unit. "I've gotten word, Mia. Marti has been retrieved."

Mia closed her eyes and nodded. She felt enormous relief. At least that part had gone right. "Thank you, Aiden."

He pulled off his comm. unit and put his mouth close to her ear. "*I wish you weren't here!*"

Mia glared at him. She didn't take off her own comm. unit. She didn't care who overheard her. "I'm the medic, remember? I've been assigned to this mission, too!"

Aiden just looked at her. He put his comm. unit back on. Stoniness settled over his features. His chiseled lips were clamped tight. He didn't have to say anything. Mia figured he was thinking about how she had made her case with the general. *Our first really big argument.* It hadn't ended in make-up sex, either. Misery weighed her down.

Aiden was still staring at her, but he didn't look angry anymore. The gaze he had locked on her had turned sad. Mia sniffed. *I am not going to cry.* She turned away from the intensity in his baby blues. She couldn't face him anymore.

She had other things to think about. Her heart thudded, hard and heavy. She was going into battle! He wasn't the only one wishing she was somewhere else, but she felt like she didn't have a choice.

Mia could feel the med kit under her fingers. Its familiarity was comforting. She hoped she wouldn't have to use it. The problem was she didn't know anymore what was supposed to happen in the movie. It had gotten all messed up. A lot of things had changed. Her being in the movie had *made* them change.

Killing off a minor character like her would be an easy way to get back on script.

If she was going to die, she wanted to be somewhere close to Aiden, instead of having a stupid accident off-screen and never seeing him again. And if Aiden's number was up, Mia wanted to be there to try and patch him up good enough so that he made it back to the field hospital.

Aiden didn't want her on the mission because he was afraid that she would get hurt. That's what they had yelled at each other about. Well, that and a couple of other things, and things that neither of them had even said. *The whole thing is stupid, stupid, stupid.* Mia felt all ripped up inside.

At least she wasn't snoring on her sofa, with television white noise buzzing in her ears and a cat curled up in her lap. For the first time in like forever, she felt intensely alive.

A voice blared in her comm. unit. "Get ready! We're moving in to target!" One of the troopers slid open the metal door. Air and noise whooshed inside.

WHUMPWHUMWHUMP

Mia didn't mind the deafening racket this time. Her hair blew around her head and the comm. unit over her ears. She held on tight to the strap above her head like she had been told. She wasn't going to be jumping out or do anything else Evel Knievel crazy. That suited her just fine. She'd stay in the nice helicopter while the troops did their thing. Her stomach was clenched so tight it ached.

On the ground, she could see the tiny figures of Cadero's men flattened against the stone walls of the commandant's fortified headquarters. They waited, guns in their hands. The hot haze of the rising sun washed over them and made them look surreal.

Suddenly, tracery bullets splat-splat-splatted from all of the helicopters. Masonry exploded from the walls of the compound. Like frenzied ants, the commandant's men scrambled along the walls, shouting and ducking. The massive doors in the wall took a direct missile hit and blew up. Shards of wood and metal burst like fireworks. Cadero suddenly leaped out of hiding and shouted, waving his men forward. He and his men plunged through the gaping, smoking hole that had been made of the doors.

The troops in Mia's helicopter leaped out on thin snaky lines, slithering towards the ground. She could see more Special Ops troopers jumping out of the other helicopters. Aiden was the first out of her helicopter. Caesar Thomas was second. Mia's heart stood still as she watched them plunge toward the earth. She didn't think she'd ever breathe again.

Pain radiated in her hand. Mia looked up. She had twisted her fingers so tight in the strap that it was cutting into them. She was glad. The pain kept her anchored. Otherwise, Mia thought she might throw up.

The special effects were spectacular, even better than Mia remembered from the movie. The firefight didn't last long. Their troops and Cadero and his men took care of the remaining resistance. The helicopter set down. Mia scrambled out, slinging her med kit over her shoulder. The airship lifted up again, heading towards the place where they would all meet up. Her hair whipped against her cheeks under the harsh whoosh of the rotor blades.

Mia ran into the compound courtyard, stumbling over the thick rubble. Smoke and dust stung her eyes. She swiped them clear but her eyes only teared up again. She looked wildly around. Then through the thick gray haze she saw a big man with a big gun striding towards her. "Mia!"

Her throat tightened. She was so glad to see Aiden that she flew into his arms. He wrapped her up tight, almost crushing her against his chest. She had never felt anything so good in her life.

Aiden set her back on her feet. He grinned at her. Mia grinned back at him. It was a perfect Technicolor movie moment. *The lovers safely reunited!* She wondered if the music score was soaring, but of course she couldn't hear it from inside the movie.

Cadero walked up. His black eyes were alight. He was grinning. There was blood splattered on his uniform and soot blackened his face. "Ah, Dr. Haven! It is good you are here! You have come to see that we are safe, yes?"

Mia laughed. She had watched her first movie battle close up. She was still alive. The adrenaline rush, mixed with high-octane fear, was still slamming through her. She felt giddy. "Yes!"

Cadero gestured wide. He looked proud. "As you can see, we do not have any casualties. We are very fortunate."

"The surprise strike was a complete success." Aiden smiled down at her. His eyes caressed her. "We sustained only minor flesh wounds. Not anything that you will need to worry about."

Mia breathed deeply and nodded. Her hands were shaking. She couldn't have applied a bandage if her life had depended on it. "That's good."

She looked around. Special Ops troops and Cadero's men moved all over the compound. She saw Caesar Thomas emerge from the cell block, escorting a skinny little man dressed in rags. He led him across the courtyard towards the blasted doors. Some of Cadero's men guarded the disarmed prisoners that huddled in a corner of the courtyard, squatting with their hands on their heads.

On the balcony above them, revolutionary soldiers shouted that they had found the commandant – cringing behind a sofa under a wall hanging! All around, there were a lot of crude comments about the commandant's lack of manhood.

"Bring him down!" shouted Cadero. Two soldiers roughly manhandled the commandant down the stairs and into the courtyard towards Cadero. The commandant's hands were tied in front of him. His hair stuck up at all angles and his uniform looked rumpled. His boots were dusty.

Mia couldn't help but remember how he had looked when she and Marti had been pushed into his office. He had been all spit and polish and shine, then. His huge wardrobe in that big clothes closet of his wasn't doing him any good now. Mia yearned to hold a colossal mirror up in front of him. Give him one good look and she bet he'd freak big time.

Cadero waited silently. There was no more laughter on his face and his black eyes had turned opaque and cold. The two soldiers stopped the prisoner before him. He stared the commandant up and down. "We meet again at last."

The commandant's face grayed. He looked shocked and a lot like he wanted to wet his pants. "*You*! But – but – You're dead!"

Cadero smiled. It was not a nice smile. He still looked sexy, though. He drew a long, long blade out of a leather sheath at his hip. The huge knife glinted silver in the sunshine. "We are going to have a very nice talk together, commandant, about my sister and other things," he said gently. He jerked his head. "Take him to the cell block."

The commandant started struggling. "No! *No!*" The revolutionary soldiers holding him dragged him away. His boots left twin trails gouged in the dirt.

Cadero turned to Aiden and Mia. He smiled broadly. His dark eyes were alight with good humor. He slammed the knife home into the leather sheath and held out his big scarred hand. "Ah, my friend! Aiden Smith! How can I thank you?"

Aiden shook Cadero's hand. Then he stepped back, adjusting the strap of his big gun over his shoulder. The black camo streaking his face made his expression hard to read. "No thanks needed, Cadero"

"But of course, I must thank you! You have given me a wonderful gift today. It is a gift that I will...enjoy...for a very long time." There was darkness underlying Cadero's voice. His eyes suddenly glittered hot. His lips tightened around his white teeth, hardening his smile.

Mia shuddered. He didn't look sexy anymore. In fact, Cadero looked a whole lot like he had looked on the big screen as he had slit an enemy's throat. It had been an impressive scene.

Cadero noticed her reaction. He laughed uproariously, pointing a big finger at her. "The little doctor does not approve! Do not fret, mi amiga. I will play the cat with the mouse for a little while only. Then I will give the commandant over to justice. My people will not be satisfied until they have their revenge, you understand?"

Mia studied Cadero's face, the way his black eyes glittered and how his white teeth were bared. She thought about that awful torture room upstairs. Her stomach roiled.

"I just want to go home," she said in a tiny voice.

"But of course! You are free to go!" Cadero waved his arm in a broad grandiose gesture. He grinned, looking sexy again. The silvery scar twisted and stood out on his brown cheek. He looked every inch the mean, lean mercenary. "Perhaps you will tell this Sly Stallone of me, yes? You will tell him how I became the Rambo of my people." He banged a fist on his broad chest. "I will be a good leader. You will see."

Mia jerked her head in a nod. She smiled sickly. All she wanted was to get away from Cadero, far, far away. In the movie, he did crazy things. Mia didn't want to find out how crazy he could get. Of course, he *was* sexy-looking. And he loved his sister. But still – she wasn't sure she would ever want to trust him to watch her back.

Aiden's hand closed on her upper arm. Mia nearly sagged with relief. "It has been an anxious day for the good doctor. I'll need a jeep and a truck for transport for us and my men to the rendezvous with our helicopters."

"It is a simple matter!" Cadero turned on his heel and bawled orders.

Within minutes, their few wounded and the rest of the troops were safely loaded in the truck. Aiden and Mia got in the back of the jeep. Caesar Thomas got behind the wheel and the mystery man got into the seat beside him. Then they drove away in a cloud of dust, leaving Cadero waving after them. He looked a heroic figure, standing in front of the blasted door of the compound. Mia watched in the side mirror as he got smaller and smaller until he finally disappeared.

Aiden sighed. He pulled her tight against his shoulder. "I hate to say it. I like the guy. But we might have to take him down someday."

Mia didn't say anything. She just sat there with her head on Aiden's shoulder.

Chapter Twelve

The mysterious man that they had sprung out of the commandant's nasty cell block was whisked off to parts unknown. Mia never heard his name. She never heard what happened to him. Aiden and Mia were taken to headquarters for debriefing. Then they went back to Aiden's place, where they showered together and made love and showered again. Then they had a long, long serious talk.

Mia knew her life would never be the same.

Mia left Aiden standing in front of his quarters. The sun struck glistening gold sparks in his hair and limned his magnificent physique. His electric blue eyes glinted. He gave a half-smile and lifted a hand in goodbye. Mia blew a kiss to him before she climbed into the waiting jeep. Then the driver gunned the engine and drove her away, rapidly leaving Aiden behind.

She didn't look back, even though she wanted to.

Marti was waiting for her at the airfield. A military helicopter was perched on its runners on the tarmac behind her. When she saw Mia in the approaching jeep, Marti grinned and waved and bounced up and down.

The driver stopped the jeep. Mia climbed out, snatching up a manila envelope lying on the seat. She ran across the intervening distance and Marti ran to meet her. They hugged and laughed, clinging to one another.

Marti was practically bubbling with excitement. "Oh, Mia! I got snatched up by a *real* Special Ops guy dangling on a line from out of a *helicopter*! It was the coolest thing ever! I'm going to learn to skydive when I get home!"

"Why would you want to *jump out*, when you know how to *fly* a plane?"

"But why *wouldn't* I want to jump out?"

"Okay, okay! Whatever!" Mia took a deep breath and let it out. She was getting distracted. "I'm glad you had some fun."

She let go of her best girlfriend and looked closely at her. Marti looked all right, just really shiny-eyed and excited. "You're really okay? I mean – with everything that happened?"

Marti shrugged. The wattage of her smile dimmed a little. "Oh, there were some scary parts, but I've kind of liked being in an action movie."

"Uh – you didn't have to *stay* in that stinking cave, did you?" Mia had really wondered about that. Given a choice, she was glad she had ended up above the cantina having heat-stroke. Then there had been Aiden – *like I can ever forget!*

"Oh, no! I was taken to a very nice hacienda, where Miguel's widowed aunts and his widowed mother and his sister all live. Oh, and his grandmother!" Marti creased her brows, her expression thoughtful. "I think all those women make him a little crazy."

"What *about* Cadero? I thought you two were getting pretty close." Mia hoped Marti wasn't hooked on him. She hoped Marti hadn't gotten her heart broken. Cadero simply wasn't good enough for her best girlfriend. He might look like a Rambo, but he wasn't.

"Miguel?" Marti got a dreamy look in her eyes for an instant. Then she shook her head. Her tone was very matter-of-fact. "He is really sweet and sexy and I really like his sister. But it's not like Miguel or I wanted more than a hot romp in the sheets. It's like having a vacation fling. It's been fun, but I'll be glad to get home."

Mia's concern for Marti, and her quick relief that she was really okay, suddenly evaporated. "Yeah, about that, Marti. About going home." Mia felt a huge lump forming. She cleared her throat. "I'm – I'm here to say goodbye. I'm staying with Aiden. He's asked me to marry him."

Marti's eyes got huge. "Mia! But you can't stay in the movie!"

"I love him, Marti." Mia left it at that. She begged Marti silently with her eyes to understand. She closed her fingers tighter, feeling the texture of thick paper beneath her grasp, and she thought about what she was holding.

Maybe she *could* stay. Surely whatever cosmic laws existed in movie land could make an exception for lovers. *Oh, come on, the movies and lovers – what could be a better match than that?* She and Aiden were willing to try and make it work, anyway. It hadn't been easy to explain to Aiden where she was really from, but he had grasped the concept surprisingly quick. He had just nodded and said that he had suspected something was different about her. *Gotta love a man like that.* And she did.

Marti stared at her. Then she slowly nodded. Her gaze dropped to the envelope Mia was clutching. She sighed. "Okay. What do you want me to do?"

"You're the best, Marti!" Mia handed the slim manila envelope to her. "My resignation letter to the hospital is in here. I wrote that I'm taking another position, one with the military. I also did a letter for my apartment complex manager. I said in it that I'm taking a position with the military and I'm being transferred and that you would handle packing up my things for me. I included a check to cover breaking my lease early. The key to my apartment is in there. I want you to have anything of mine that you want. You can get rid of everything else."

Marti nodded again. There were tears sparkling in her eyes. Her mouth was trembling. She didn't seem able to say anything.

Mia smiled a shaky smile at her. Her own eyes were misting, making everything swim in front of her. When Mia started to tell her the rest, her voice got husky. "And I want my best girlfriend in the whole world to be my maid of honor at my wedding."

"*Ooh*, you are such a *jerk*! You've made me *cry*!" Marti sobbed and gulped and sobbed some more as she grabbed Mia in a fierce hug. Mia laughed and hugged her back and cried, too.

A soldier walked up to them and snapped a salute. He looked appreciatively at Marti. Even when she cried, she looked gorgeous. "Ma'am, you're to come with me. I'm to get you back to the contact point."

Mia and Marti clung together for another minute; then slowly, reluctantly, they parted. They tried to smile at each other. Marti stepped further back. She tilted her head as she looked at Mia. Her eyes were like twin lasers. "You're good?"

Mia nodded. She grinned. "Yeah, I really am."

"Okay, then."

Marti and the soldier started walking towards the waiting helicopter. The rotor blades were rotating and kicking up a dusty swirl. Mia shouted, "You'll always be my best girlfriend!"

Marti got a huge grin and waved. Then she disappeared into the black maw of the helicopter. The blades whirred faster and faster until they blurred, and the motor roared. The helicopter launched upwards into the sky. Mia watched it become smaller and smaller, until it completely disappeared.

Mia turned and climbed back into the waiting jeep. "Lieutenant Smith's quarters, driver." She sat back and smiled, even as tears spilled down her face.

Chapter Thirteen

Aiden solemnly stared at his best friend. Caesar stared back. They both were attired in crisp dress uniform as the current operation demanded. It was the most somber, most monumental task they had ever embarked on. It had to go off with complete precision. Nothing could be left to chance. Every detail had been worked out. There was no room for omission or oversight. Aiden slid into full-blown jitters. *It's a cluster bomb waiting to go off.*

"Are you sure about this, Aiden? No one's twisting your arm."

Aiden swallowed. He was point-man. His heart pounded and he was beginning to sweat. His belly was clenched, just like before any other important operation. He took a deep, fortifying breath. His hands were actually shaking. He'd never been more uncertain or frightened in his life! But he had volunteered, confident it was the right thing to do. He still thought it was the right thing. He couldn't back out now, even if he wanted to and he absolutely did not!

He would not be entering the field on his own. *We're a solid team.* Remembering that gave him the steadying boost of confidence he needed. All at once his nerves settled. Setting his jaw, he nodded. "I'm sure!"

Caesar took a deep breath of his own. He didn't smile, but he gave a reassuring nod. "I've got your back. You know that."

"Right!" Aiden nodded again. He didn't need to ask, because he trusted Caesar to come through, but he did anyway. "Have you got the article in safekeeping?"

Caesar patted his uniformed breast. "Right here."

"Then let's do this!"

THE WEDDING WAS MOVIE-perfect. It was held outdoors on a sunlit white beach with palm trees swaying in the breeze and the boom of the turquoise blue ocean in the background. It looked like a pretty postcard.

Naturally, as the bride, Mia was beautiful. She wore a gorgeous Victorian-style champagne and lace wedding gown, low cut and nipped in at the waist and flared at the hips. She hadn't known before how to describe her kind of figure, but now she did. It was hour-glass perfect and in her bridal gown she was a real bombshell. At least, Aiden looked like he had been hit by a bomb when he saw her, so that was good enough for her.

A humid breeze gently ruffled her hair, but she wasn't worried. She knew her hair wouldn't frizz. She also knew her make-up was perfect, making her look like a sultry starlet. Underneath her wedding gown, her Victoria Secret white push-up bra did very nice things for her bosom. She wore a silky wisp of a slip and under that, a matching white lace thong, garters and white stockings. Mia felt incredibly beautiful and sexy. Her secret fairy godmother had sprinkled extra magic movie dust over her.

Aiden was wearing his dress uniform. It fit him like a glove, the tailored coat outlining the proud line of his broad shoulders before it arrowed down over his flat stomach and lean hips. The tight crisp pants had a military stripe running down the outside of each leg. He could have been the poster boy for Prince Charming.

There were a whole lot of people dressed in uniform attending the wedding. An army chaplain was performing the ceremony. The general, uniformed chest bristling with medals, solemnly gave Mia away. When she kissed his leathery cheek, he turned red but he looked proud.

Her very best girlfriend in the world was her maid of honor. Marti was dressed in a lovely frothy frock that swirled around her with every gust of breeze. When Aiden's best man, Caesar Thomas, first saw her, his mouth dropped open. Then he scowled and smoldered her with his dark eyes. Marti pretended not to see him, but Mia saw her look at him from under her lashes.

Mia noticed that more than one hot, male military gaze was fixed on Marti.

Mia didn't mind. She knew Marti was prettier than her, but Mia only needed one man's gaze and he was looking only at her. There was love in his electric blue eyes and he had a sexy grin on his face. Mia peeped under her own lashes. *God, the man can wear a uniform! I might make him keep it on and smear streaks of black camo on his face tonight.*

Happy, naughty fantasies whizzed through Mia's mind. At really the most inappropriate time in the ceremony, Mia was thinking about Aiden pulling her white lace thong off with his teeth and – She couldn't stop grinning.

Aiden glanced down at her as he slipped the diamond-studded gold band on her finger.

Mia looked deep into his eyes and fluttered her lashes. Heat flared in his baby blues. Delighted, she watched his jaw tighten. Then he gave her the slowest, sexiest smile. Mia could feel his gaze slide like molten honey down her nicely showcased cleavage. She shivered in delicious anticipation. She knew he was reading her mind. She had such bad, bad thoughts, too.

Mia still couldn't believe it. She had Aiden Smith, her very own and very hot action-hero! Yes, she did mean hot as in *hot. Keep the red glass slippers, Toto. I won't need them.*

Aiden kissed her. He swooped her up, bent her back over his arm, and planted a hot one on her. His mouth seared hers in the plundering kiss. Mia forgot all about cute little dogs or anything else. She was blown away by heat and sizzling desire. When he let her go, she was so dizzy her head was spinning.

Mia dimly heard a lot of clapping and military huzzuhs. The only thing that mattered was Aiden's deep laughter and the warm strength of his muscular arm wrapped around her waist. She dreamily smiled up at him. The sea breeze caressed her hair and ruffled the long skirt around her legs. She was giddy with gladness. The boom of the ocean was the perfect counterpoint to her fast-beating heart.

The movie's music score had to be soaring.

Happiness bubbled through her. Someone put a chilled champagne flute in her hand and Mia looked at the golden effervescence. Then she laughed and laughed. Her whole body shook. Tears came to her eyes. *Who needs champagne for fizzy bubbles?*

Beside her, Aiden cracked up. It was like doing the wave. Spontaneous laughter broke out all over, some people even doubling over as they whooped.

Afterwards, renewed congratulations were shouted out and there was a flurry of back-slapping of the groom and honorary kissing of the bride. Marti surged toward Mia, both hands outstretched. She laughed and cried all at once as she caught Mia in a tight hug. "I'm going to miss you!"

"I'm going to miss you, too!" Mia hugged her back, just as tightly. Then she whispered in her ear. "See you at the movies!"

When Marti stepped back, her eyes had grown very wide. "*Seriously?* I mean, do you really think so?"

Mia grinned at her, happiness zipping through her. "Aiden is getting a promotion! He's going to be permanently attached to intelligence and I'm going to be working at the base field hospital! I'll bet he gets sent off on some real action hero missions. I'll probably tag along as a field medic. What do you think?"

Marti wailed. "Oh, Mia! You *know* how much I hate action movies!" Her eyes were bright and shining. "I'm going to buy all of the DVDs!"

Then together, they laughed.

Don't miss out!

Visit the website below and you can sign up to receive emails whenever Kate Anthony publishes a new book. There's no charge and no obligation.

https://books2read.com/r/B-A-JJSJ-HAZCB

BOOKS2READ

Connecting independent readers to independent writers.

Also by Kate Anthony

Action Hero Fan Girl